Ace Fixed His Blue Eyes On Her, And Maggie Knew She Was Dealing With A Man Who Was Accustomed To Having His Way.

It would be so easy to knuckle under to him.

Easier still to be seduced by him.

A whimper from the baby reminded her why she could afford to do neither.

Stiffening her spine, she set her jaw. "You need to understand something."

"What's that?"

"No man touches me without my permission."

"Oh, I'll remember," he assured her, "but the same doesn't go. In fact, you can touch me anytime, anywhere, and you won't hear a complaint out of me."

He bumped his knuckle against her chin to close her gaping mouth, then shot her a wink, turned and strode from the room.

Maggie stood rooted to the spot, staring at him until he'd disappeared from sight.

Touch him anytime, anywhere?

"Oh, God," she moaned. "What have I gotten myself into?"

Dear Reader,

Welcome to another stellar month of stories from Silhouette Desire. We kick things off with our DYNASTIES: THE BARONES series as Kristi Gold brings us *Expecting the Sheikh's Baby* in which—yes, you guessed it!—a certain long-lost Barone cousin finds herself expecting a very special delivery.

Also this month: The fabulous Peggy Moreland launches a brand-new series with THE TANNERS OF TEXAS, about *Five Brothers and a Baby,* which will give you the giddy-up you've been craving. The wonderful Brenda Jackson is back with another story about her Westmoreland family. *A Little Dare* is full of many big surprises…including a wonderful secret-child story line. And *Sleeping with the Boss* by Maureen Child will have you on the edge of your seat—or boardroom table, whatever the case may be.

KING OF HEARTS, a new miniseries by Katherine Garbera, launches with *In Bed with Beauty*. The series focuses on an angel with some crooked wings who must do a lot of matchmaking in order to secure his entrance through the pearly gates. And Laura Wright is back with *Ruling Passions,* a very sensual royal-themed tale.

So, get ready for some scintillating storytelling as you settle in for six wonderful novels. And next month, watch for Diana Palmer's *Man in Control*.

More passion to you!

Melissa Jeglinski

Melissa Jeglinski
Senior Editor, Silhouette Desire

Please address questions and book requests to:
Silhouette Reader Service
U.S.: 3010 Walden Ave., P.O. Box 1325, Buffalo, NY 14269
Canadian: P.O. Box 609, Fort Erie, Ont. L2A 5X3

Five Brothers
and a Baby
PEGGY MORELAND

Silhouette® Desire

Published by Silhouette Books

America's Publisher of Contemporary Romance

SILHOUETTE BOOKS

ISBN 0-373-76532-0

FIVE BROTHERS AND A BABY

PEGGY MORELAND

published her first romance with Silhouette in 1989 and continues to delight readers with stories set in her home state of Texas. Winner of the National Readers' Choice Award, a nominee for the *Romantic Times* Reviewer's Choice Award and a two-time finalist for the prestigious RITA® Award, Peggy's books frequently appear on the *USA TODAY* and Waldenbooks bestseller lists. When not writing, you can usually find Peggy outside, tending the cattle, goats and other critters on the ranch she shares with her husband. You may write to Peggy at P.O. Box 1099, Florence, TX 76527-1099, or e-mail her at peggy@peggymoreland.com.

One

The room the Tanner brothers gathered in was like everything in Texas. It was *big*. Rough-hewn logs felled and notched by the first Tanner to settle in the Texas Hill Country in the 1800s framed three sides of the room; a stone fireplace, broad and deep enough to barbecue a whole steer, spanned the fourth. Photographs framed in tooled leather covered the walls, depicting the family's climb in both prosperity and power.

Though considered large even by Texas standards, the room seemed to shrink in size as the current generation of Tanners filed inside. Death had brought the brothers together again, but it was duty that bound them now. Duty to a father who had single-handedly driven them away with his careless and wild ways from the home and ranch where they were raised and, ultimately, from each other.

Ace, the oldest, seated himself behind their father's desk, assuming the position as head of the family—a job, he knew, his brothers were more than willing to relinquish to him. Woodrow, four years Ace's junior, took a seat on the leather sofa opposite the desk, while Rory, the youngest, dropped down on the opposite end. Ry, the second-born, paced.

His expression grim, Ace met each of his brothers' gazes in turn. "I guess y'all know he's left us one hell of a mess to deal with."

Woodrow snorted. "So what's new?"

Ace nodded, understanding his brother's sarcasm. "The old man did seem to thrive on stirring up excitement."

Rory, the most laid-back of the four, stretched out his long legs and folded his hands behind his head. "Excitement, hell," he drawled. "*Trouble* would be more like it."

Ry stopped pacing to shoot his brother a quelling look. "There's no need to be disrespectful. This *is* our father we're talking about."

"And just about everybody else's in the county," Woodrow muttered under his breath.

Though Woodrow's comment was an exaggeration, not one of his brothers challenged him on it. With his tomcatting ways and his secretiveness, the old man could have populated a town twice the size of Tanner's Crossing and they never would have known it.

"Ry's got a point," he said, hoping to steer the conversation back toward the purpose of the meeting. "We're not here to judge the old man. Our job is to untangle the mess he's left us with."

Ry glanced impatiently at his watch. "Then let's get on with it. I need to get back to Austin. I've got a full surgery schedule in the morning."

Woodrow snorted a breath. "And we certainly wouldn't want to keep the good doctor from making another million or two, now would we?"

Primed for a fight since the day he'd arrived, Ry lunged

for Woodrow, caught him by the lapels of his Western suit and dragged him to his feet.

Rory jumped up to separate the two. "Come on, guys. You can beat each other's faces in later. Right now we've got business to tend to."

Ry glared at a Woodrow a full second, then gave him a shove that sent him sprawling back on the sofa. Ace nailed him there with a steely look, before he could leap back up.

"The old man didn't leave a will," Ace said, hoping to refocus his brothers' attention on the business at hand, before another fight broke out. "So it's going to take awhile to settle the estate. In the meantime, we've got a ranch to run."

Ry whipped his head around. "We?" he repeated. "I can't work the ranch. I'm a surgeon. I've got a practice to maintain."

"We *all* have other obligations," Ace reminded him. "But it's going to take all of us, chipping in what time we can, to keep this place going. At least, until we decide if we're going to sell it."

Woodrow shot to his feet. "We can't sell the Bar-T! This is Tanner land and always has been."

"And hopefully it'll remain Tanner land," Ace told him. "But we won't be able to make that decision until the estate is settled and we know what we're dealing with, both financially and legally."

Sobered by the reminder that their father was as secretive about his business dealings as he was his personal life, Woodrow and Rory sank back down on the sofa.

Ry crossed to frown out the window. "What about Whit?" He glanced over his shoulder at Ace. "He should be in on this."

"I left him a message on his machine, asking him to meet us here. If he gets it in time, he'll come."

Woodrow grunted. "He didn't show up for the old man's funeral. What makes you think he'll come here?"

"Why should he?" Ry returned. "The old man treated him like dirt."

"Whit was at the funeral."

Woodrow turned to look at Rory. "Where? I didn't see him."

"That's because he didn't want to be seen."

Chuckling, Woodrow shook his head. "That damn kid. He always was a sneaky little bastard."

"Quiet," Ry corrected. "Not sneaky."

"Is that a professional diagnosis?" Woodrow shot back. "And here I thought you were a plastic surgeon for the rich and famous, not a psychiatrist."

Though Ry tensed at the verbal jab, he didn't respond to it, an act of control that Ace would thank him for later. With all they had to deal with, both known and unknown, Ace knew fighting among themselves would only complicate matters more. He quickly directed the conversation back to the purpose of their meeting.

"Since I'm currently between photo assignments, my schedule is the most flexible, so I'll stay here at the ranch until the estate is settled. But I can't run the ranch alone. I'll need all of you to pitch in. We'll need to—"

The doorbell chimed, interrupting him, and Ace pushed to his feet. "That's probably Whit now."

"More likely a neighbor coming to pay their condolences," Woodrow grumbled, unwilling to let go of his anger.

Ace stopped in the doorway and slowly turned back around. "Whoever it is," he said evenly, "I expect the three of you to be on your best behavior. Understood?"

Woodrow and Rory rolled their eyes and looked away, but Ry met Ace's gaze squarely almost defiantly, as if to let Ace know he wasn't a little kid any more who could be bossed around by his big brother.

Pushing a disgusted hand at the lot of them, Ace headed for the front entry, praying it was Whit at the door, so they could get this business settled once and for all. The sooner he could get away from Tanner Crossing, the better. Being on the ranch again and in the town named for his family, was already beginning to wear on his nerves.

But when he opened the door, instead of his stepbrother Whit, he found a woman standing on the porch. Dressed in faded jeans and a bright blue T-shirt, she clutched a blanket-wrapped bundle against her chest—a bundle that looked suspiciously like a baby. Ace glanced behind her at the beat-up car parked on the drive. Not recognizing the woman or the vehicle, he peered at her curiously. "Can I help you?"

"You can, if you're one of the Tanner brothers."

The bitterness in her voice surprised him. This was no neighbor coming to offer her condolences, that was for sure. "Ace," he informed her, and stepped out onto the porch. "Ace Tanner. The oldest. And you are?"

"Maggie Dean."

He stole a glance at the blanket-wrapped bundle, then shifted his gaze back to hers. The defiant gleam in her eyes immediately put him on guard. "And what business do you have with the Tanner brothers, Ms. Dean?"

She shoved the baby at him. "I'm bringing you what's yours."

Ace fell back a step, shooting his hands up in the air. "Whoa. Wait a minute. That baby's not mine."

"By law it is."

"What law?" he snapped, suddenly impatient.

"Any law."

"Now just a damn minute. I—"

A wail rose from the depths of the blanket and Ace winced at the irritating noise.

The woman tipped up a corner of the blanket. "There, there, precious," she soothed. "Everything's all right. He wasn't yelling at you."

Ace planted his hands on his hips. "Look, lady," he said, having to raise his voice to make himself heard over the crying infant. "I don't know who you are or why you chose to stop here, but that is *not* my baby." He pointed to her car. "Now, you get yourself and that squalling brat of yours off Tanner land, before I call the law."

She jerked her chin up, her face flushed with fury, her eyes blazing with it. "I'll be happy to get off your land, but the baby stays."

With that, she thrust the crying infant against Ace's chest. He caught the bundle instinctively as the woman whirled away. Stunned, he stared after her. Something struck his chest and he glanced down to find two tiny fists had worked free of the blanket and were flailing the air. As he watched, the folds of the blanket parted and a miniature-sized face appeared, its features too small and too perfect to be real. Vivid blue eyes leaking crystal tears that glimmered in the sunlight; a little pink nose no bigger than one of the buttons on his shirt; a tiny circle of a mouth, open birdlike.

But the sound pouring from that tiny mouth was certainly real enough.

He looked up again to find the woman had made it to her car and was jerking items from the backseat and tossing them out onto the grass. "Hey!" he yelled. "What are you doing? You aren't leaving this kid here."

She slammed the car door and turned, shoving the strap of a large duffel bag over her shoulder. "She's not a *kid,*" she said through clenched teeth. "She's a *baby.*" She stooped and grabbed the handle of some of kind of contraption, then straightened. "And she *is* staying."

Since anger had gotten him nowhere with the woman, Ace tried reason. "Look," he said, struggling for patience. "Obviously you're in trouble and need help." He shifted the baby to one shoulder and held it there as he worked his wallet from his rear pocket. He flipped it open one-handed and held it out to her, revealing a thick wedge of bills tucked inside. "Take what you need. Take all of it, if you want."

She slapped his hand away, sending the wallet flying from his grasp. "You're just like your father," she accused bitterly. "You think money solves everything. Well, it doesn't! What this baby needs is family. Someone to take care of her, to love her."

Ace's mind registered nothing after the word *father*. Suddenly he felt weak, sick. "This is my father's baby?"

"Yes, she's your father's!" she cried. "That's what I've been trying to tell you since you opened the door."

Ace hauled in a breath, trying to still the dizzying sensation that threatened to force him to his knees. "My father's," he repeated.

She pursed her lips. "Yes, your father's."

Ace caught her by the arm and dragged her to the porch. "We need to sit down. Talk about this."

She stumbled after him, the portable playpen knocking against her legs, impeding her movement.

When he reached the porch, Ace pushed her down onto a step, but changed his mind about sitting, as well. Instead, he paced, absently thumping a wide hand on the baby's back. He didn't bother to ask the woman for proof that the infant was his father's. It was a wonder this scenario hadn't taken place before.

But Ace was at a loss as to what to do. He'd never had to deal with his father's indiscretions before. In the past, if one of the old man's lady friends, as his father referred to the women he became involved with, kicked up a fuss and started making demands the old man dealt with them himself...and usually by buying the woman off.

"If it's a matter of money," he began.

Groaning, the woman dropped her forehead against her hands and fisted her fingers in her hair. "I've already told you I don't want your money. What I want is for you to give this baby a decent home."

"Hell, you're the kid's mother! You give it a home."

She jerked up her head, her hands balled against her thighs. "She's not a *kid*. She's a *baby*. And I'm *not* her mother."

Ace stared, more confused than ever. "Then who is?"

Dropping her gaze, she rubbed the heels of her hands up and down her thighs. "Star. Star Cantrell."

"So why doesn't she provide a home for the kid?" he demanded to know, his anger spiking again.

"She's dead."

She said it so softly, Ace wasn't sure he'd heard her correctly. But then he saw a fat tear drop to splatter on the back of her hand. "Dead?" he repeated.

She nodded, then dashed a hand across her cheek, wiping at the tears. "Yes. A little over a week ago. Something went wrong after the birth. She began to hemorrhage and—" She waved away the explanation, as if the cause of death wasn't important. Not any longer. "I worked with Star. At the Longhorn. We were...friends. She made me promise if something happened to her, that I'd bring the baby here. Give her to your father."

She forced a swallow, then shook her head. "I didn't want to. I'd met your father. But I'd promised Star. Then I heard that your father had died. I wanted to keep her myself, but—"

She looked up then, and Ace wished she hadn't. He

couldn't remember ever seeing a face more ravaged by grief, by regret in his life.

She lifted a hand, then let it fall helplessly. "I can't keep the baby." She dropped her gaze and shook her head. "She deserves more than I can give her. That's why I brought her here."

Ace stared, aware of the faded jeans the woman wore, the work-reddened knuckles of the hands she held fisted against her thighs, the beat-up car she arrived in. What the woman was saying was that she couldn't afford to keep the child. "Surely there's someone else," he said. "Star must have had family somewhere. A mother. Sister. Aunt. Somebody."

She shook her head. "No. She was an only child. Her parents died in an automobile accident when she was a teenager."

Before he could think of another solution, she pushed to her feet.

"Everything you'll need is here," she said, gesturing at the duffel and portable playpen. "Diapers. Bottles. Formula. Clothing. She sleeps in the playpen, though you'll probably want to get her a crib fairly soon."

She turned to look at him…or rather, at the baby, and tears flooded her eyes. "Star named her Laura. I hope you won't change it. That's the only thing she'll ever have that was given to her by her mother."

Ace looked down at the baby, only now aware that the infant had stopped crying. She slept, one cheek turned against his shoulder. The lashes that brushed the upturned cheek were spiked with tears.

When he lifted his head, the woman was gone. He spun and ran after her, trying not to jostle the baby overmuch. "Hey! Wait!"

She turned, one hand on the door handle of the old car.

He stopped, breathing heavily, more from panic than exertion. "Listen. I know this isn't your problem, that you're just doing what you were asked to do, but you can't leave this kid here. My brothers and I all have jobs, careers, responsibilities. We can't take care of a baby. We wouldn't even know how to begin."

He watched her face as she shifted her gaze to the baby, seeing the hesitation, the uncertainty, her obvious affection for the infant. Then she firmed her lips and pulled open the car door.

"You'll figure it out," she said, as she slid behind the wheel and started the engine. "I did."

Ace grabbed for the door. "No! You can't—"

Before he could demand that she take the baby with her, she stomped down on the accelerator and sped away, ripping the handle from his grasp.

The slam of the door reverberated through Ace like a death knell, as he watched the car disappear from sight.

Maggie made it five miles down the road, before she was forced to pull to the shoulder, blinded by tears. Giving in to them, she dropped her forehead against the back of her hands and wept. She wept for the baby who would grow up without ever knowing her mother. For Star, the baby's mother, and a life cut so tragically short.

And she wept—selfishly, she knew—for the loss of the baby she'd grown so attached to, for the inequities in life that made it impossible for her to keep the child herself. And while she wept, she sent up prayers, beseeching God to look after the baby, to keep it safe. To soften the hearts of the Tanner brothers so they would accept the baby into their home and into their lives.

When she was done, when there were no more tears to be shed, she tugged the hem of her T-shirt from the waist of her jeans and mopped her face, blotted her eyes. Then, with a sniff, she put the car in gear and pulled back onto the road.

It's best this way, she told herself, as she made the drive home. She had a hard enough time keeping a roof over her own head and food in her belly to even consider taking on the responsibility of an infant. With the Tanners, Laura would have a chance at a better life. They had a castle-size home, butt-loads of money and even a town named after them. With them, Laura would never have to worry about being evicted for late rent payments, where the money for medical expenses would come from or whether she could afford to go to college. And she'd have the opportunity to socialize with people with real class and not have to live around the kind of scum Maggie had lived with all her life.

But there was one thing that Maggie knew she could have given Laura in spades.

Her love.

The four Tanner brothers flanked Ace's bed, two on each side, staring down at the baby Ace had placed in its center.

Ace glanced over at Ry. "Take her with you to Austin. You're the one with a wife."

"Ex-wife," Ry reminded him. "Or soon will be."

Scowling, Ace looked at Rory. "What about you? Couldn't you get one of the ladies who works in your chain of Western stores to baby-sit for awhile?"

Rory shook his head. "No way. It's summer and vacation time. I'm already down to a skeleton staff as it is."

He looked back across the width of the bed at Woodrow.

Woodrow held up a hand. "Uh-uh. Don't even ask. The only experience I've had with babies was when my dog Blue had a litter of pups."

Ace tossed up his hands. "Well, what the hell am I supposed to do with the kid? I don't know any more about babies than the rest of you."

Ry gave him a pat on the back, as he turned to leave. "You can handle it."

"Yeah," Woodrow agreed, backing from the room. "You always were good at handling things, Ace."

Ace clamped a hand on Rory's arm, stopping his brother before he could follow the other two from the room. "Where do you think you're going?"

"Uh...to get the baby a bottle? Yeah, a bottle. She's probably hungry."

Ace slowly relaxed his grip. "All right. But make it fast. I don't want her to start crying again."

"Sure thing, bro," Rory promised...then turned and ran.

Ace heard the front door slam behind all three of his brothers, the rev of three engines.

And swore.

Bleary-eyed, Ace jostled the squalling infant on his shoulder as he watched the pan, willing the water to boil.

"Come on, kid," he begged pitifully. "Give me a break. I'm doing the best I can."

When the baby only cried louder, he snatched the bottle from the pan, shook a couple of drops of milk onto the inside of his wrist, testing the temperature, then used his foot to drag a chair out from the table.

Easing down, he shifted the baby to cradle in the crook of his arm and stuck the bottle in her mouth. She latched on to the nipple and sucked, as if she hadn't eaten in a week, which he knew wasn't the case, since she'd gotten him up a minimum of three different times during the night to give her a bottle.

With the baby occupied for the moment—and quiet—he reached for the phone book and drew it to the edge of the table, desperate to find someone to take care of the kid. He'd already called every child care facility listed in the Yellow Pages and been told by each that they didn't accept newborns. His only hope was to locate the woman who'd dumped the kid on him in the first place and try to hire her.

And he'd do that just as soon as he remembered her name.

It started with a D, he recalled, and was short. He quickly flipped pages to the D section and began to skim. Daily. Dale. Davis. Day. Dean. That was it! Dean. Maggie Dean. Relieved, he skimmed the listings, searching for her name, but didn't find anything that came even close. Unwilling to give up, he pushed aside the phone book and reached for the portable phone. He quickly punched in the number for directory assistance.

"Information. May I help you?"

"I hope so," he said with a weary sigh. "I'm looking for a listing for Maggie Dean." He frowned when the operator asked for the city. "I don't know. Some place in Texas, I'd guess."

While he waited, he thumbed a line of milky drool from the corner of the baby's mouth and wiped it down the leg of his jeans.

"I have a listing for a Maggie Dean in Killeen."

Recognizing the town as one near Tanner Crossing, Ace went almost weak with relief. "That's bound to be her." He tucked the phone between shoulder and ear, while he grabbed a pencil.

As he wrote down the number, it occurred to him that it might be better if he talked to Maggie face-to-face, rather than over the phone, figuring it would be harder for her to refuse him in person.

"Do you have an address?" he asked. He jotted that down, as well, then thanked the operator for her help and punched the disconnect button.

"Well, kid," he said, pleased with himself. "Looks like we're fixing to take us a little ride through the country."

*   *   *

To say Maggie lived in a low-rent district would be an understatement, Ace thought, as he drove slowly down her street.

Wood-framed houses lined the narrow, potholed road, each less than spitting distance from its neighbors. Junk cars were parked along the curb and on the postage-stamp-sized lawns, while cast-off furniture and appliances seemed the decorative choice for sagging porches.

As he searched the fronts of the jammed-together houses for her address, he found himself remembering the clunker of a car she had driven, the worn jeans, her work-roughened hands.

He spotted the faded numbers of the address he'd jotted down and pulled to the curb in front. Like the other cookie-cutter houses surrounding it, it was sorely in need of repair. Peeling paint; missing shingles; a silver strip of electrical tape stretching across a broken windowpane. A sidewalk shot in a straight line from the street to the porch. Halfway up to the house there was a hump in the walk where the concrete had broken and the parched earth had forced it to buckle.

But unlike the neighboring houses, no cars were left abandoned on Maggie's lawn. No ratty furniture or rusted appliances cluttered her small porch. Though her attempts at improving the place were meager, the pride she took in her home was obvious. A sprinkler turned lazily beneath an already blazing sun, casting badly needed water over clumps of newly planted plugs of grass. From the porch eaves hung wire baskets filled with a colorful array of cascading flowers. On the front door, a wooden sunflower with the word Welcome hand-painted in the flower's center greeted guests.

Ace tried to name the emotion that suddenly crowded his throat. Pity? No, he thought. Not pity. It was more an over-

whelming sadness at her feeble attempts to make the dump
a home. Which was stupid, he told himself, as he reached
to unbuckle the seat belt from around the infant carrier. He
didn't want to feel anything for this woman but relief when
she agreed to return to the ranch with him and take care of
the kid.

He hooked an arm around the car seat and climbed down
from his truck. Silently praying he could convince Maggie
to see things his way, he strode for the front door. He
rapped his knuckles on the wood just above the Welcome
sign, then shifted the carrier to a more comfortable position
on his hip and waited. The faint sound of music came from
somewhere inside. Country, he noted with relief, not that
god-awful heavy metal so many favored these days.

The door opened and he quickly stuck a foot in the opening before she could slam it in his face.

Narrowing her eyes at him through the crack that remained, she kept a firm grip on the door. "What do you
want?"

"Your help." When she tried to shut the door again, he
put a shoulder against it. "Please. Just hear me out."

She glared at him for a good five seconds, then dropped
her gaze, noticing the infant for the first time. She gulped,
staring, then set her jaw and released her hold on the door.
"Make it fast," she said, as she turned back into the
room. "I have to go to work."

Ace quickly pushed his way past the door, before she
changed her mind about letting him inside. "Ten minutes,
max," he promised. He glanced around, noting the cleanness,
if scantiness, of her furnishings. "Mind if I sit down?"

Folding her arms beneath her breasts, she tipped her head
toward the sofa beneath the front window, but kept her lips
pressed tightly together. Her silence didn't worry Ace. He
planned on doing most of the talking anyway. He plunked

the carrier down on the sofa, then rolled his arm, lengthening the cramped muscles, before dropping down beside it.

Stretching his arms out along the sofa's back, he focused his gaze on her. Another time, he might have taken a moment to admire the length of long legs exposed by the short denim shorts and the swell of breasts beneath the red bandanna print cropped shirt, but at the moment he was more interested in finding a baby-sitter for the kid than he was the anatomy of a good-looking woman. "I've got a proposition for you."

"If you're here to try to persuade me to take the baby, you're wasting your time. I've already told you I can't keep her."

He shook his head. "No. Actually, I came to offer you a job."

She rolled her eyes. "I have a job. Now, if you don't mind—"

Ace held up a hand, cutting her off. "Just hear me out. My brothers and I are willing to take responsibility for the ki—" At her arched brow, he amended quickly, "I mean baby. But, as I said before, we're just a bunch of bachelors and don't know the first thing about caring for an infant. The obvious solution, as far as I can see, is to find a relative of Star's who'd be willing to take the baby in. I plan to hire a private detective to track down Star's family, but in the meantime…" He lifted his hands. "Someone's got to take care of the baby."

"And you want me to be that someone."

"You seem the perfect choice. You obviously developed an affection for the baby while you had her, and you're already familiar with her routine."

"I have a job," she reminded him. "Plus, I go to college part-time. I don't have the time or energy to take on anything else."

"I'm not asking you to. What I'm proposing is that you quit your job, take a break from your classes. Work full-time for me. As a nanny of sorts." He watched her face and was sure that he saw a change in her expression. Interest? "How much money do you make as a waitress?" he asked.

Her chin came up. "That's none of your business."

"I wasn't being nosy. Just trying to establish a base. How about if I offer to pay you say…six hundred a week."

Though she didn't say a word, he could tell by the rounding of her eyes that his offer was a hell of a lot more than she currently earned waiting tables. "And free room and board," he added, hoping to sweeten the pot a little more. "Does that sound like a fair offer to you?"

He watched her throat convulse in a swallow and knew she was close to saying yes. In hopes of tipping her over the edge, he pulled his cell phone from his shirt pocket and tossed it to her. "Call your boss. Tell him you quit. We can use my truck to haul whatever you want to take with you to the ranch."

She slowly flipped open the cover of the phone. She'd punched in at least four numbers, before she stopped. "I can't."

He pushed out a hand, urging her to complete the call. "Sure you can. Once you've given your notice, we're outta here."

"But what happens to me if you're able to locate Star's family? I'll be out of a job." Pressing her lips together, she snapped the cover on the cell phone back into place. "I won't do it. Jobs are too hard to come by. You'll have to find someone else."

Ace leaped to his feet. "Dammit! There isn't anyone else! I've already called every child care facility in town and was told they don't take newborns."

Awakened by Ace's shouting, the baby began to whimper. He dropped his head back and groaned. "Please, don't start squalling again," he begged. "My nerves can't take any more."

In the blink of an eye, Maggie had tossed aside the phone and was across the room, snatching the baby from the car seat.

"She's been crying?"

"Yeah," he said cautiously, watching her. "Most of the night."

Her face creased with worry, she gently laid the baby on the sofa and began to examine her. "Did you feed her?"

"Yeah. Three or four times."

"Change her diaper?"

He shuddered upon being reminded of that disgusting task. "Yeah. And she's definitely not constipated, if that's what you're worried about."

Maggie picked up the baby and held her against her shoulder, as she began to pace. "Did she sleep at all?"

"Some, I guess. At least, I assume she was sleeping, when she wasn't screaming."

Maggie continued to pace, while frantically patting the baby on the back. "It's okay, precious," she soothed. "Maggie's got you now."

Ace watched, kicking himself for not thinking of just handing over the baby when he'd first walked in the door, instead of waving money in front of Maggie's face. It appeared the kid was much more of an inducement than a big salary.

There was a loud burp and Maggie jerked to a stop to look at the baby in surprise. She turned slowly, narrowing her eyes suspiciously at Ace. "Did you burp her?"

"Burp her?"

"Yes. At least twice while she was having her bottle."

He lifted a shoulder. "Didn't know I was supposed to."

"Seven hundred."

Ace looked at her confusion. "What?"

"Seven hundred a week. And I'll need at least one day off."

Though he hoped this was the last time he ever had to touch the kid, Ace pried the baby from Maggie's arms. "Seven hundred it is." He nodded toward the cell phone she'd dropped. "Now why don't you make that call so we can get this kid home before she needs another feeding."

Maggie took the baby right back from him. "No. I'd rather give my notice in person."

"How long will that take?" he asked in frustration.

"I don't know. A half hour or so. But there's no need for you to wait." She clutched the baby tighter against her chest. "Laura can ride along with me."

Two

When a woman doesn't own much, it doesn't take her long to pack. Maggie completed the task within fifteen minutes of Ace's departure. Within thirty, she was standing in front of the Longhorn Restaurant and Saloon, the baby in her arms, taking one last look at the place she'd worked for the past four years.

After sundown, when the oversized neon horns above the entrance were lit and the parking lot was jammed full of vehicles, the Longhorn didn't look half bad. But in daylight, with the cracks on the stucco facade as glaring as varicose veins on an aging woman's legs, and the sidewalk and the parking lot littered with empty beer cans and debris, it looked shabby, cheap.

But Maggie was used to shabby and cheap. She'd lived with both all her life. She intended to see that Laura didn't have to do the same.

Pressing a kiss against the top of the baby's head in a

pledge to fulfill that promise, she headed for the rear of the building. Finding the delivery door locked, she used her key to enter. The hallway she stepped into was dark, as were the kitchen and public rest rooms she passed, but ahead she could hear Tammy Wynnette's soulful whine coming from the jukebox in the bar. She followed the sound and found Dixie Leigh, the Longhorn's owner, perched on a tall bar stool, studying her liquor order for the day, her eyes squinted against the thin column of smoke curling from the tip of the cigarette she held clamped between her teeth. With her bottle-red hair teased high, false eyelashes and skin tight jeans, Dixie looked much the same as the building she owned—faded and cheap.

But beneath the layers of heavy makeup and too-tight clothing, Maggie knew lay a heart of solid gold.

"Hey, Dixie," she called softly.

Dixie jumped, then snatched the cigarette from her mouth and scowled. "Girl, don't you know how to knock? You almost made me swallow this thing."

Biting back a smile, Maggie approached the bar. "Shouldn't smoke."

"Shouldn't do a lot of things," Dixie grumbled, "but there you are." She shifted her gaze to the baby, her frown deepening. "I thought you took that kid to the Tanners?"

"I did. Ace brought her back this morning."

"Ace? He'd be Buck's oldest. The wildlife photographer."

"He didn't mention his line of work."

Dixie grunted. "Guess he was too busy dumping the kid and hightailing it to take time for any small talk. A shame, too, since all the Tanner men are blessed with such pretty faces."

Maggie couldn't vouch for all the Tanner men, but if the rest of them looked anything like Ace, they'd been blessed with more than just pretty faces. They had the bodies to go along with them. "I really didn't notice," she said vaguely.

Scowling, Dixie tamped out her cigarette. "Which is more the shame." She fluttered her fingers, motioning for Maggie to bring her the baby. After settling the infant in the crook of her arm, she lifted the blanket back from its face. Her lips trembled as she looked down at the sleeping infant. "Ain't she just the prettiest little thing," she murmured. "The spittin' image of her mama."

Maggie heard the tears in Dixie's voice and felt her own throat constrict. "Yes, she is."

Dixie shook her head with regret. "Seems like I should've been able to do something to prevent all this. The minute Star walked into the Longhorn, I knew that girl was headed for a bad end. Had tragedy written all over her."

"She needed a job and you gave her one," Maggie said in her employer's defense. "What Star did with her free time was her choice and no fault of yours."

Dixie sighed wearily. "I suppose." She stared down at the baby a moment longer, then glanced up at Maggie. "So you're going to keep her, after all?"

"Oh, Dix. You know I can't."

"Then what are you going to do with the child?"

Maggie avoided Dixie's gaze, knowing her employer probably wouldn't approve of her plans. "That's what I came by to talk to you about."

Dixie narrowed her eyes. "Why do I get the feeling that I'm not going to like what you have to say?"

Maggie lifted a shoulder. "Probably because you're not."

"Well, you might as well spit it out," Dixie snapped irritably. "Dragging out the telling isn't going to make it any easier for me to swallow."

"Ace has asked me to work for him as Laura's nanny."

For a moment, Dixie could only stare. "You're quitting your job here?"

"I'd rather think of it as taking a leave of absence," Maggie said, hoping to soften the blow—and at the same time leave a door open for herself should she need it. "If you'll let me, I'd like to come back once Ace locates Star's family."

"Star didn't have family," Dixie reminded her drolly.

"No," Maggie agreed. "At least, not that she mentioned to us. But Ace is convinced she has a relative somewhere. An aunt or a distant cousin, maybe, who'd be willing to take the baby. He's hiring a private detective to track them down."

"And you think this private eye's gonna find someone?"

Maggie shook her head. "I think if Star had any family, she would've told me."

"Then why are you letting the Tanners waste good money chasing folks who don't exist?"

"They can afford it. Besides, it'll give Laura some time."

"Time for what?"

"To win them over." Curving a hand around the top of the baby's head, Maggie smiled down at the sleeping infant. "A few weeks with this sweet little angel and they won't be able to let her go."

"Ace has already told you they don't want her."

"No," Maggie corrected, straightening. "He said they didn't know how to take care of a baby. With me there to see to her needs, that won't be a problem."

Dixie eyed her suspiciously. "You see yourself in this kid, don't you? You think by sticking with her, you can prevent happening to her what happened to you."

Maggie stiffened defensively. "I'm only doing what Star asked me to do."

"You've already done what Star asked of you. You delivered her baby to the Tanners."

"She asked me to take the baby to Mr. Tanner. His death made that impossible."

"So you did the next best thing. You delivered the kid to his heirs. And what about your schooling?" Dixie went on, not giving Maggie time to argue. "You've worked too hard toward that nursing degree to give up on it now."

"I'm not giving it up. Once things are settled for Laura, I can pick right up where I left off."

Her expression melting to one of concern, Dixie cupped a hand on Maggie's cheek. "Oh, honey. I know you're only trying to do what's best for the baby. But if you don't cut your ties to her now, you're going to get your heart broke for sure. And, God knows, you've had it broken enough times as it is."

Gulping back tears, Maggie closed her hand over Dixie's and held it against her cheek. "I'm just giving her a chance, Dix. The same as you gave me."

Dixie pressed her lips together. "I gave you a job when you were down on your luck. Nothing more."

"You gave me a lot more than a job. You gave me back my pride, my self-confidence, the opportunity to make something of myself."

Dixie snatched her hand from beneath Maggie's. "I gave you a *job,*" she repeated stubbornly. "Whatever else you've done with your life, you've done on your own."

"I couldn't have done anything, if you hadn't given me a break when I needed it. And that's what I want to give Laura. She deserves a decent home and a shot at a halfway normal life. With the Tanners' name and money behind her, she'll get both."

Dixie eyed Maggie, her lips pursed in annoyance. "You've already made up your mind about this, haven't you?"

"Yes."

She eyed her a moment longer, then heaved a sigh of defeat. Sliding an arm around Maggie's waist, she hauled her up hard against her side. "Then you be careful, you hear? Those Tanner men can be dangerous."

"Dangerous?" Maggie repeated in alarm.

Dixie drew her arm back to tuck the blanket beneath the baby's chin. "Not in the way you might think. But a handsome face and a smooth tongue can be as deadly a weapon as any gun."

"You don't have to worry about me," Maggie assured her. "My only interest in Ace Tanner is his ability and willingness to provide Laura with a decent home."

Dixie humphed. "For now, maybe," she conceded grudgingly. "But mark my words. Before this is over, you'll be singing a different tune. I've yet to meet the woman who didn't fall head over bloomers for a Tanner, once he took a notion to seduce her."

Ace sat reared back in his father's chair, his boots propped on the desk's oak surface, the phone held loosely at his ear, as he briefed his stepbrother Whit on the meeting he and his brothers had held the day before.

"Since the old man didn't leave a will," he finished, "we've got a hell of a mess to sort through."

"I don't know why you're telling me all this. Even if the old man had left a will, he wouldn't have named me in it."

Ace heard the bitterness in his stepbrother's voice and understood it. What Whit said was true. The old man probably wouldn't have included him in his will. Buck Tanner might've adopted Whit, but he'd never treated him as a son.

But, in Ace's mind at least, Whit was a Tanner and would inherit his share of the old man's estate, the same as Ace and his brothers would. By *not* leaving a will, the old man had unknowingly given Ace the opportunity to right some of the wrongs Whit had suffered at the old man's hand.

"But he didn't leave a will," Ace reminded him pointedly. "Which means that his estate will be split equally between his heirs. Since he adopted you, by law you're entitled to a full fifth."

"I don't care what the law says," Whit said stubbornly. "I want nothing that was his."

"Now, Whit," Ace began.

"No," Whit said, cutting him off. "I'll do what I can to help y'all settle the estate, but not for any personal gain."

Ace knew it would be a waste of his time to press the issue…for the moment, at least. But Whit would get his fair share of the old man's estate, as would the half-sister he'd known nothing about. Ace would see to that.

"I appreciate your offer of help," Ace told him, opting to focus on the positive portion of Whit's reply. "We can certainly use it."

"Well, you've got it, though I don't know how much help I'll be. I know next to nothing about the laws pertaining to estates."

"It isn't your legal advice we need," Ace assured him. "We've got a string of attorneys on retainer to handle that. What we need is your help here on the ranch."

"Why? The ranch hands ought to be able to handle whatever needs to be done. They've been working on the place for years."

"What ranch hands?" Ace said wryly. "The bunkhouse is empty and has been since the day I arrived."

"What?" Whit said, sounding surprised. "The hands wouldn't just up and leave because the old man died. Not when there's livestock needing tending."

"I wouldn't have thought so, either," Ace replied. "But

the fact is, they're gone. You knew most of the men who worked here. Maybe you can do some checking. See if you can track them down, persuade them to come back.''

"Hell, Ace. You know how cowboys are. They drift with the wind. No telling where they are by now.''

"If anybody can find them, you can.''

"Maybe,'' Whit said doubtfully. "But it's liable to take me awhile.''

Ace frowned. "Unfortunately, we don't have a lot of time. God only knows where the cattle are or what condition they're in.''

"Dry as it is, I'd imagine they've scattered, searching for grass and water.''

"Yeah, I'd imagine so,'' Ace agreed. "I'm planning to ride out this afternoon and—'' The chime of the doorbell had him lifting his head. "Hang on a minute, Whit,'' he said into the receiver. "Somebody's at the door.'' He clamped a hand over the mouthpiece and yelled, "Come on in! It's open!'' then drew the phone back to his mouth.

"Like I was saying,'' he said, continuing his conversation with Whit. "I'm riding out this afternoon to see if I can locate any of the herds.'' He glanced up and saw Maggie hovering uncertainly in the doorway. With the car seat balanced on one hip and her shoulder weighted down by a large duffel bag, she looked more like a pack mule than a nanny…although Ace couldn't remember ever seeing a pack mule built quite like Maggie was. Still dressed in the getup she'd had on earlier, she could've easily posed as a model for one of the cowgirl pinup calendars he'd seen in Rory's store.

He hesitated a moment, debating whether he should jump up and hug her for showing up as promised or tell her he'd changed his mind about hiring her to take care of the kid. Having a good-looking woman in the house might present more problems than it solved, and Ace had enough problems to deal with at the moment.

One glance at the baby convinced him that he'd rather take his chances on another problem arising, than have to deal with the kid.

He waved Maggie in and pointed to the sofa. "Keep me posted on how many of the ranch hands you're able to locate," he said to Whit. "If you have to, promise them a bonus to get them to sign back on with the Bar-T."

"Sure thing, Ace."

"In the meantime, we're going to have to round up the herds and see what kind of shape they're in. Plan on meeting here at the ranch, say, a week from Saturday at daybreak. That'll give me a good ten days to get a handle on things around here. I'll call Ry, Woodrow and Rory and let 'em know we're gonna need their help, too."

Ace opened his mouth to say something else, but Maggie chose that moment to bend over and set the car seat on the sofa. He totally lost his train of thought as he watched the denim shorts ride up higher on the back of her thighs, accentuating the cheeks of a well-shaped butt and legs that seemed to stretch on forever. His mind dulled by the view, he said to Whit, "I'll be in touch," and broke the connection.

As he leaned to replace the receiver, Maggie straightened, moaning softly, her hands pressed low on her back. Letting the strap of the bag slide down her arm, she hunched her shoulders to her ears, then turned and sank down on the sofa with a weary sigh.

Her change in position put Ace at eye level with her chest and an interesting—if miserly—peek of cleavage. Disappointed that the cropped shirt wasn't cut a little lower, he lifted his gaze higher and found her looking at him through narrowed eyes.

Since he'd been caught red-handed, Ace didn't see much

point in trying to deny his guilt. He lifted his hands. "What can I say? I'm a healthy, red-blooded, all-American male."

Reaching behind her, she gave the shirt a tug, snatching the top up higher on her chest. "That's the lousiest excuse for voyeurism I've ever heard."

He shrugged. "A woman wears an outfit like that, a man is bound to look."

She gave her chin an indignant lift. "It's my uniform. All the girls at the Longhorn are required to wear them."

"Let me guess," he said, having to bite back a smile. "The Longhorn's clientele is predominantly male."

"Killeen's a military town, so the men outnumber the women just about everywhere you go. But if you're thinking the Longhorn's some kind of titty bar," she was quick to inform him, "you're wrong. Dixie serves up the best chicken fried steak in Texas and books the most popular country and western bands the area has to offer. *That's* what draws the men to the Longhorn. Good food and good music. Not the waitresses."

If the woman thought food held more appeal to a man than the scantily-clad women delivering it, Ace didn't see why he should be the one to tell her otherwise. Keeping his expression impassive, he leaned back in the chair and laced his fingers over his middle. "This Dixie sounds like an astute businesswoman."

"She's that and more."

"Did she give you any trouble about quitting on such short notice?"

"No, but I didn't actually quit. I asked for a leave of absence, instead. That way, once I'm done here, I'll still have a job."

He snorted a laugh. "You don't believe in burning any bridges, do you?"

She shrugged. "Can't afford to. Like I told you before, jobs are hard to come by."

Her comment brought to mind her broken-down car and the rundown neighborhood she lived in, which made him wonder about her background. He'd been so desperate to get her to agree to come to the ranch and take care of the baby, he hadn't asked anything about her personal life, an oversight he figured he should rectify before they went any further.

"Since you were able to pick up and leave so quickly, I assume you're not married."

She gave him a withering look. "A little late for an interview, isn't it, since you've already hired me for the job?"

"Just trying to get to know you a little better. What's the harm in that?"

Though he could tell she resented doing so, she complied.

"Single white female. Twenty-eight. Divorced. No hobbies. Not looking for male companionship, sexual or otherwise." She lifted a brow. "And you?"

Since she'd tossed his question right back at him, Ace responded in the same personal-column-ad manner in which she'd revealed her stats.

"Single white male. Pushing forty. Divorced. Enjoy fishing and hunting when I have the time." He waited a beat, then added with a wink, "And I'm *always* looking."

He wasn't sure why he'd tossed in that last bit, but considering the attitude she was sporting, he would've sworn it would've gotten a rise out of her. When she remained silent, her gaze steady on his, he cleared his throat and plowed on. "So…who wanted out of the marriage? You or your ex?"

"I guess I'd have to say he did, since he was the one who left, taking with him our only means of transportation and owing three months back rent."

Ace puckered his lips in a silent whistle. "Nice guy."

"Yeah. A real angel. Who gets the blame for yours?"

"Mutual agreement." At her doubtful look, he held up a hand. "Swear to God. Though the official decree states irreconcilable differences as grounds for the divorce."

"That's certainly original," she said dryly.

"The judge who granted the divorce didn't seem to have a problem with it."

"I doubt he would, you being a Tanner and all."

Ace stiffened at the insinuation. "And what's that supposed to mean?"

She lifted a shoulder. "From what I've heard, your family practically owns the town. I'd imagine they own the politicians, as well."

Her interference to the Tanners' power in the town hit a nerve. A sore one. "The Tanners don't own Tanner's Crossing," he informed her, to set the record straight. "Yes, we own several businesses and substantial real estate holdings here, but we do not own the town."

"Then why is it called Tanner's Crossing?"

"Because it was a Tanner who settled here first, and Tanners who built the town." Hoping to distract her from pursuing the subject further, Ace steered the conversation away from his family and back to her. "You said you were going back to work at the Longhorn, once we've located Star's family."

"If you find any."

"Everybody's got relatives."

"I don't. But even if Star does, there's no guarantee that whoever you find will want to take her baby."

Ace had thought about that possibility—and promptly discarded it, not wanting to think about what that would mean to him and his brothers. For some reason, hearing Maggie voice the possibility annoyed the hell out of him. "Are you always this pessimistic?" he asked irritably.

She lifted a shoulder. "Just thought I should point out what problems you might encounter."

Scowling, he dropped his feet to the floor and stood. "Well, don't. I've got enough trouble to deal with, without you borrowing more."

At the mention of trouble, Maggie tensed. "Trouble?" she repeated, keeping her gaze on him as he rounded the desk. "What kind of trouble?"

He picked up her duffel and turned for the door without responding. She hopped up and grabbed the car seat, hitching it on her hip as she charged after him.

"What kind of trouble?" she asked again, having to trot to keep up with his longer stride.

"None that concerns you."

She firmed her lips. "Look, Slick. If I'm going to be living with you, I think I have a right to know if you're in some kind of trouble."

"There aren't any warrants out for my arrest, if that's what you're worried about."

"And that's supposed to make me feel better?"

Heaving a sigh, he turned to face her. "It's more like problems than trouble. The old man left us with a butt-load of 'em, not the least of which is a ranch to run and no ranch hands to do the work."

"What happened to the ranch hands?"

"That's the million-dollar question."

"Your father never said anything to you about firing them or them quitting?"

"The old man and I never talked."

Her eyes rounded in amazement. "Never?"

"Never."

"Why not? I mean, he *was* your father. Seems like you would've at least checked up on him every now and then, especially considering his age and the fact that he lived alone."

"Buck Tanner was healthy as a horse and more than capable of taking care of himself."

"Well, he couldn't have been all that healthy," she said wryly. "He died, didn't he?"

"Of a heart attack, which I couldn't have prevented even if I'd been here."

"But you were his son," she persisted. "Didn't you worry about him at all?"

"Look. If all this is to make me feel guilty, you're wasting your breath. Not where the old man is concerned. Now if you don't mind," he said, and tipped his head toward the door on his left. "I've got things to do."

Not at all satisfied with the answers he'd given her, Maggie gave him a sour look as she passed by him. Two steps beyond the threshold, she stopped short, her eyes rounding, as she got her first look at the room he'd shown her to. It wasn't luxurious. Not by modern-day standards. But it was the most beautiful room she'd seen outside the covers of a decorating magazine.

Opposite her, a four-poster mahogany bed, covered with an heirloom-quality, hand-crocheted spread, stood between two floor-to-ceiling windows. Angled in the corner was a chaise lounge upholstered in a dusty pink velvet, an ecru chenille throw draped across its back. To her left, a porcelain pitcher and bowl rested on the marble top of a washstand. On her right, a tall linen press stretched almost to the ceiling. Beside it was an open doorway through which she could see the tip end of a old-fashioned footed tub. All the furnishings appeared to be genuine antiques, probably passed down from one generation of Tanners to the next.

And Maggie intended for Laura to be a part of the next generation of Tanners to enjoy this rich heritage.

"If you don't like this room," Ace said from behind her, "there are others."

She swung her head around, having forgotten his presence. "Oh, no," she said quickly, then slowly turned back to stare. "It's just that it's so—" She laid her palm over the dainty roses covering the cream-colored wallpaper. "Feminine," she finished, unable to think of a better word to describe the room.

He strode by her and dropped her duffel at the foot of the bed. "My stepmother's doings. And before you ask why I haven't asked her to take care of the baby, she's deceased, killed by a drunk driver years ago. As to the decorating," he went on, "she claimed she had to have one room in the house with a little fluff, since she was forced to live in an all-male household outfitted more like a hunting lodge than a home. Threatened us within an inch of our lives if we put so much as a foot inside."

Figuring a woman would have to be pretty tough to issue an ultimatum like that and expect a houseful of males to obey, Maggie crossed to the washstand and ran a hand lightly over the marble surface. Surprised at the amount of dust she gathered, she held up her hand to show Ace. "Did her warning include the housekeeper?"

He shrugged. "I figure the housekeeper left about the same time as the ranch hands. The whole place could stand a good cleaning."

She dragged her palm across the seat of her shorts. "I'll take care of it."

"Now wait a minute," he said. "I wasn't suggesting that you take on the cleaning chores. I hired you to take care of the baby. Period."

"I don't mind. Besides, it'll give me something to do while Laura naps."

He eyed her a moment, as if wanting to argue, then sighed and gestured to the adjoining bath. "Towels are in the linen closet. Extra pillows and blankets are on the top shelf of the closet. If you're hungry, there's plenty of food left over from the funeral meal in the refrigerator. If you need anything else, you can make a list and give it to me later.'' He turned for the door. ''I'm saddling up and riding out to see if I can locate any of the cattle. Probably be gone most of the afternoon.''

''I'll need Laura's playpen,'' she called after him. ''She'll want a nap soon.''

''It's in my room. I'll get it.''

While Ace went after the playpen, Maggie set the car seat on the bed and lifted the baby out. Unable to resist, she dropped a kiss on the infant's cheek before laying her down on the bed. Cooing softly to the baby, she unwound the receiving blanket from around her legs. Laura kicked and waved at the air, obviously enjoying the freedom of movement, after being confined in the infant carrier for so long. Laughing at her antics, Maggie glanced up as Ace returned, carrying the playpen.

''Look,'' she said. ''She's doing aerobics.''

He glanced the baby's way, as he set the playpen at the foot of the bed and frowned. ''Needs to. I've seen bigger legs on a malnourished bird.''

Maggie caught the baby's foot and placed a kiss on her toes. ''Don't you listen to him,'' she lectured gently. ''He's just jealous because your legs are prettier than his.''

''Since you've never seen my legs, how would you know?''

Smiling down at the baby, Maggie pressed a finger lightly to the end of the infant's nose. ''I wouldn't. But I've seen your eyes and Laura's are the same shade of blue.''

''All babies' eyes are blue,'' he muttered disagreeably, but eased closer for a better look.

Taking his curiosity as a sign of interest, Maggie decided this might be the perfect time to start establishing a relationship between the two. ''Not necessarily. Do your brothers have blue eyes?''

"Yeah. Except for Whit. His are brown. But he's a step-brother, so I guess he doesn't count."

"Stands to reason then that Laura's will be blue, too." Scooping the baby up, she held her along the length of her arms, angling her so that Ace had a better look. "What about her nose?" she asked, studying it thoughtfully. "Do you think she has the Tanner nose?"

When he didn't immediately reply, she glanced over and saw that he was looking at her and not at the baby. His frown told her that he'd seen right through her act.

"Don't even try," he warned.

Feigning innocence, she turned away to lay the baby back on the bed. "Try what?"

"To make me feel a connection to the kid. It's not going to work. No amount of family resemblance is going to persuade me to keep her."

When she didn't reply, he hooked a knuckle beneath her chin and forced her face around to his. "Understand?"

Maggie knew he expected a response from her. But for the life of her, she couldn't seem to push the one-syllable word past her lips. Not when his face was so close to hers she could count the squint lines that fanned from the corners of his eyes.

Dixie was wrong, was all she could think. There was nothing pretty about *this* Tanner's face. Pretty was reserved for mild-tempered men, with dimpled cheeks, who spent their evenings playing the piano for their mothers.

Ace was handsome. Yes. She couldn't argue that. But his was a rugged handsomeness, heightened at the moment by the dark stubble of beard that shadowed his jaw and the steely blue eyes leveled on hers.

When she didn't immediately respond, he increased the pressure on her chin, tipping her face up a fraction higher, as if to remind her he was waiting for—and expected—an answer. Though the movement was subtle, she sensed the strength behind the finger that held her face to his, the stubbornness in the blue eyes fixed on hers, and knew she was dealing with a man who was accustomed to having his way.

It would be so easy to knuckle under to him, she thought, feeling herself weakening.

Easier still to be seduced by him.

A whimper from the baby reminded her why she could afford to do neither.

Stiffening her spine, she set her jaw. "I understand perfectly. But you need to understand something, too."

"And what's that?"

She closed a hand over his wrist. "No man touches me, without my permission."

She felt a swell of satisfaction at the surprise she saw flare in his eyes...but it was short-lived.

"Oh, I'll remember," he assured her, biting back a smile. "But the same doesn't go. In fact," he said, "you can touch me anytime, anywhere and you won't hear a complaint out of me."

He bumped his knuckle against her chin to close her gaping mouth, then shot her a wink, turned and strode from the room.

Maggie stood, rooted to the spot, staring after him until he'd disappeared from sight.

Touch him anytime, anywhere?

Because the image of doing so came much too easily to mind, she sank down on the side of the bed and buried her face in her hands.

"Oh, God," she moaned. "What have I gotten myself into?"

Three

By the time Maggie had finished feeding the baby and putting her down for her nap, she'd convinced herself that Ace had said what he'd said to drive her crazy.

…you can touch me anytime, anywhere…

Why else would he say such a thing, if not to drive her nuts?

And if that was his purpose, he'd certainly done a good job of it. Twice, while feeding the baby, she'd actually caught herself imagining doing what he'd suggested. Framing her hands at his face and tracing the sharp ridge of his sculpted cheekbones with the tips of her fingers. Smoothing her palms over those strong, broad shoulders. Splaying them over the muscled expanse of his chest, the hard, flat plane of his abdomen.

The images alone were enough to have her thinking of sweaty bodies and tangled sheets.

Which was exactly what he'd hoped her reaction would be, she was sure.

Furious with herself for letting him get to her so easily, she snatched up her duffel and marched to the linen press to unpack.

It wasn't as if she hadn't known that something like this could happen, she reminded herself as she jerked clothes from her duffel and stuffed them into drawers. She knew that sharing a house with a man required a careful balancing act in order to keep the relationship platonic and the two from toppling into bed together.

Especially, it seemed, when the man was a Tanner.

Not that Maggie had had any personal contact with the Tanner brothers prior to delivering Star's baby to their ranch. But she'd certainly heard enough stories about them from the women who hung out at the Longhorn to know they were legends in this part of Texas. According to the gossip, they were all rich, handsome and eligible—three traits that apparently made them irresistible to the female population, considering the number of women who had claimed to have slept with one or more of them.

But Maggie had no intention of being charmed out of her panties by a Tanner. She'd let lust overrule good sense once in her life and she certainly didn't intend to make that mistake again. Lust she'd learned to deal with. And she'd learn to handle Ace Tanner, too, she promised herself, as she stuffed her empty duffel into the bottom of the linen press. It was just a matter of keeping her mind focused on her purpose for being in his home...*and* keeping a safe distance from him.

Confident that she could accomplish both, she changed from her waitress uniform into a pair of jeans and a T-shirt. With nothing else to do until the baby awoke, she decided to explore the rest of the house. She felt a moment's unease at snooping around without asking Ace's permission first, but dispensed with it by telling herself that since she'd offered to clean the house, she'd need to be familiar with its layout.

As she wandered from room to room, she began to understand what had motivated Ace's stepmother to claim a space as a feminine escape for herself. The house *did* have the look and feel of a hunting lodge, just as Ace had claimed. Though there were gorgeous antiques scattered throughout, the bulk of the furnishings and accessories leaned toward a more rustic, western-style. Most of the upholstered pieces were covered in leather, varying in hue from warm golds to dark, distressed browns, while others sported western print fabrics, as did many of the throw pillows tossed about. The art she found displayed on the walls and tabletops ranged from bronze statues of cowboys galloping on horses to priceless oil paintings of Texas landscapes to ornately carved silver objects.

And over it all lay a thick layer of dust.

Some might find the prospect of cleaning such a large house daunting, if not depressing. But not Maggie. She'd never had much, and what she did have she'd picked up at garage sales, tag sales and a few successful Dumpster dives. The thought of putting the shine back on a house like the Tanners'…well, for her, it would be more pleasure than work.

Anxious to get started, she headed for the kitchen. Obviously added on by one of the later generations of Tanners, the kitchen appeared to have undergone a fairly recent remodeling and offered every modern convenience imaginable. A brick arch above a commercial-sized range complemented the home's rustic theme, giving the appliance the look and feel of a working fireplace. Terra-cotta Mexican tiles covered the floor, while dark slabs of slate spanned the countertops. A long island, topped with butcher block on one end and beautifully veined granite on the other, created a convenient food prep area.

Dazzled by the grandeur of it all, Maggie crossed to the built-in refrigerator to check out its contents, assuming she'd be responsible for the cooking, as well as the cleaning. Her chin nearly hit the floor when she saw the number of covered bowls and casserole dishes crammed onto the shelves, apparently the leftovers from the funeral meal Ace had mentioned. Certain that she wouldn't have to cook for a month, she closed the door and rolled up her sleeves, ready to get to work. She attacked the kitchen first, using the cleaning supplies she unearthed from beneath the farm-style sink.

An hour later, with only the floor left to be mopped, she took a break to check on the baby. Finding the infant still sleeping peacefully, she returned to the kitchen and gave the tile floor a good scrubbing.

Just as she was putting the mop away in the mudroom, she caught a glimpse of Ace through the window, walking back toward the house. Wondering why he was on foot instead of horseback, she crossed to the window to peer out.

He certainly doesn't look much like a wealthy playboy, she thought with more than a little resentment, as she watched his approach. He looked more like a rough and tumble cowboy, returning home after a long cattle drive. The slow ambling gait with just a bit of a swagger. The dust-covered boots and jeans. The sweat-stained cowboy hat pulled low over his brow. If his face was visible, she knew it would only enhance the image more. With his flint-like blue eyes and sharply defined features, he could easily play the part of a gunslinger from the Wild West. All that was needed to complete the picture was a holster riding low on his hips and a six-shooter gripped in each hand.

Finding the sight of him a little too appealing, she turned away with a sniff of disdain. As she did, out of her peripheral vision, she saw him stumble. Frowning, she moved back to the window and watched as he shoved back his hat and dragged his arm across his brow. Noticing that the shirt sleeve was torn, she stepped to the door and pushed it open.

"Ace?" she called uncertainly. "Are you all right?"

At the sound of her voice, he dropped his arm and looked up. Her breath caught in her throat, when she saw that blood smeared half his face and dripped from his chin. Forgetting her vow to keep a safe distance, she flung open the door and flew down the steps, across the yard.

By the time she reached him, he was bent over, his hands braced on his knees, gulping air. Fearing he was about to pass out, she slid an arm around his waist to support him. "What happened?" she asked in alarm.

He dragged in air through his nose, puffed his cheeks and slowly blew the breath out through his mouth. "Horse spooked. Pitched me off a mile or two back. Had to walk home."

"Are you hurt?"

He pressed a hand gingerly against his rib cage. "Don't know," he said, wincing. "Might've busted a rib or two."

"And you walked home?" she cried in dismay, then clamped her lips together. "Never mind," she said, and urged him into motion. "We need to get you inside before you fall flat on your face."

He tried to shake free of her hold. "Never fainted in my life," he grumbled.

She tightened her grip on him. "Well, you better hope you don't start now, because I'm sure as heck not carrying you."

She managed to get him to the back door and used her hip to hold it open, while she maneuvered him inside. Once in the kitchen, she half pushed, half dragged him to a chair at the table and eased him down. Dropping to her knees between his sprawled legs, she looked up to examine his face more closely. Beneath the dust and blood, high on his left cheek was a puncture-type wound the size of a bullet hole.

"There's a contusion beneath your left eye."

He lifted a hand to the spot and flinched, when his finger touched the broken skin. Setting his jaw, he shook his head. "Some antibiotic cream and it'll be okay."

She pursed her lips. "That's going to need more than antibiotic cream." She reached for his hand. "Let me see your arm."

He tensed, watching as she carefully peeled back the tattered sleeve, exposing more blood and dirt and two more deep cuts.

"I must've landed on a rock or something when my horse pitched me," he mumbled.

She closed her eyes, gulped, then forced them open again. "We need to get you to a doctor."

He yanked his arm from her grasp. "No way. You're not hauling me to a sawbones over a couple of scrapes."

"These are more serious than scrapes," she argued. "You have two lacerations on your arm, one of which will likely require stitches. And that gash on your cheek might, too," she added, shifting her gaze to frown at it. "Plus, you said you might've broken a couple of ribs. You'll need X-rays to be sure."

He reared back in the chair, lengthening his chest in an obvious effort to relieve the pressure on his ribs. "Probably just bruised. There's a first aid kit in the mudroom. Top drawer of the chest. Get it for me, would you?"

She wavered uncertainly, wanting to refuse, but finally pushed to her feet, knowing it would be a waste of her time.

"You have to be the stubbornest man I've ever had the misfortune to meet," she muttered, as she strode for the mudroom.

"If you'd met my brother Woodrow," he called after

her, "You wouldn't say that. Woodrow, now he wrote the book on stubborn."

She returned with the first aid kit. "If he did," she said, as she passed by him on her way to the sink, "he had a handy case study in you." After filling a bowl with water, she knelt in front of him again, positioning the bowl and first aid kit on the floor beside her. "Take off your shirt."

"Is that an invitation or an order?"

She glanced up, surprised by the teasing in his voice. But she saw the shadow of pain that clouded his blue eyes, the deep lines of it that etched his mouth and knew that his teasing was nothing but a ruse to hide how much he was truly hurting.

It was in Maggie's nature to soothe, to heal. If he were anyone else, she would have reached up and brushed back the lock of damp hair that had fallen across his forehead, gently thumbed away the dust that had gathered in the squint lines that fanned from the corners of his eyes and teased him right back.

But this was Ace Tanner she was dealing with. The man who had given her his permission to touch him anytime, anywhere. Remembering that—as well as how tempting she found that offer—she dropped her gaze and opened the first aid kit.

"An order," she replied stiffly, as she began to lay out the supplies she'd need.

Eyeing her warily, he tugged the tail of his shirt from his jeans. "I hope the hell you know what you're doing."

"I'm training to be a nurse, so I've had some experience dealing with scrapes and bruises."

He shrugged the shirt from his shoulders, grimacing as he eased his injured arm from the tattered sleeve. "A nurse, huh?" he said, sweat popping out on his brow. "What is it they say about nurses? They do it with patients?"

Maggie recognized his need to keep talking as yet another means of distracting himself from the pain. She might have responded to that need, if he hadn't chosen that moment to drop his shirt, exposing the most incredible chest she'd ever seen in her life. A mat of dark hair swirled tightly around his nipples and arrowed down his flat stomach to disappear behind the waist of his jeans.

Tearing her gaze away from the tempting sight, she plunged a cloth into the bowl of water, struggling to find the detachment she needed to respond.

"'Nurses call the shots.' 'Nurses do it with gloves on.'" She looked up and gave him what she hoped was a patronizing smile. "You can save the jokes. I've heard them all."

"I'll bet you haven't heard this one. 'Nurses are here to save your ass, not kiss it.'"

Kiss his ass? Oh, Lord, she thought. She didn't dare even think about that! Sure that her cheeks were flaming, she dropped her gaze to his arm and frantically began to cleanse the dirt and debris that clung to the wound. When she was sure she could speak without stammering like a fool, she laid the cloth aside and picked up the bottle of antiseptic. "As a matter of fact, I've considered having that one embroidered on my nurse's cap when I graduate."

He snorted a laugh, then choked on it when she tipped the bottle over his arm, flushing out the cuts. "Damn!" he swore. "That stuff burns like hell."

She blew to cool the stinging sensation. "Better a little discomfort than an infection."

He closed his free hand over the edge of the chair's seat as if prepared to endure whatever tortures she had planned for him. "Spoken like a true medical professional," he grumbled.

"It's a required class for all nursing students. Handy Retorts for Whiners 101."

Tipping his head back, he closed his eyes. "Handy Retorts for Whiners," he mumbled, then chuckled weakly. "If it isn't a class, it ought to be. I'd imagine a nurse takes a lot of grief from her patients.''

"Sometimes. But nursing can be a very gratifying career, too.''

Puzzled by her comment, Ace lifted his head to peer down at her. "How would you know if you've never worked as one?''

She pulled a strip of tape over the cut, measuring the length she needed to close the wound. "I've done volunteer work as a nurse's aid in the hospital. An internship for one of my classes,'' she explained, then warned, "this might hurt a little.''

Clamping his teeth together, he watched as she pulled the torn flesh together and applied tape over it. He was surprised to find that, in spite of her prickly and sour disposition, she had the touch of an angel. "What made you want to be a nurse?''

She measured off another strip of tape. "Taking care of my mother before she died. She didn't have insurance and had to rely on indigent care. The staff at the hospital where she was admitted was less than courteous to her and sometimes careless with the medical treatments they dispensed.'' She lifted a shoulder, as she pressed the strip into place. "I guess they figured since she couldn't afford to pay, she didn't deserve the same quality of care as those who could.'' She lifted her shoulder again. "Anyway, that's when I decided to become a nurse.''

Ace thought of his own mother's hospital stays during her brief but painful fight against cancer and the five-star treatment she'd received there, and suspected that Maggie was right. "How old were you?'' he asked curiously.

"Sixteen.''

"Wow. Your mother must've died awfully young.''

"She was thirty-one.''

"Thirty-one!" he exclaimed. "But that would've made her—"

"Fifteen when she had me," she finished for him, then looked up and met his gaze squarely. "And, no, she wasn't married."

Judging by the defiant gleam in her eyes, Ace figured she was a bit touchy about her illegitimacy. "I don't recall asking whether she was married or not."

She dropped her gaze and pressed the last strip into place. "Most people do."

Ace stared at the top of her head, feeling a bit guilty because the question had been on the tip of his tongue to ask. Though he wanted to quiz her more about her mother, he decided it best, considering her touchiness, to keep his questions to himself. "So you've wanted to be a nurse since you were sixteen," he said instead.

She wound the gauze back onto the roll. "That's right."

"If you knew what you wanted to do with your life, what took you so long to begin your studies?"

She stretched to place the gauze back inside the first aid kit. "Money. Circumstances."

"What kind of circumstances?"

She rocked back on her heels to look at him in frustration. "What is this? Twenty questions?"

"Just curious."

Pursing her lips, she bent to gather the bowl and cloths. "My ex thought boozing it up with his buddies was more important than me getting an education."

Not wanting to answer any more questions about her past, Maggie rose and headed for the sink.

She took her time rinsing out the cloths and refilling the bowl with fresh water, but when she turned, she found that Ace was watching her, his eyes narrowed thoughtfully.

Uncomfortable, she looked away as she crossed back to

the table and set down the bowl. "If you'll lean your head back and close your eyes, it'll make this a lot easier."

Though she half expected him to grill her with more questions, he tilted his head back and closed his eyes. Breathing a quiet sigh of relief, she eased closer to examine the cut.

Confronted with the dried mixture of dust, sweat and blood that covered most of his face, she wished that she'd had the forethought to insist that he take a shower before she began treating his wounds. And a good shampooing wouldn't have hurt, either, she thought, shifting her gaze to his hair. Thick and jet-black, it lay plastered against his head, flattened there by the cowboy hat he'd shoved off when he'd first sat down.

Cupping a hand at the back of his neck to hold his head in place while she cleaned his face, she paused, her heart softening a bit, as she looked down at him. A part of her yearned to comb her fingers through his thick, dark hair, lift the wayward lock that had fallen across his forehead and smooth it back into place.

Another wiser part knew what a mistake that would be.

Forcing herself to focus on the task at hand, she pulled the cloth from the bowl, squeezed the water from it and began to wash his face. She gently wiped the cloth across his forehead and down his cheek, removing as much of the blood and dirt as possible without causing him any more pain. As she drew the cloth along the line of his jaw, she couldn't help but notice again how prominent his features were, what a manly ruggedness they added to an already handsome face. The thick dark eyebrows. The high slash of cheekbone. The strong, square jaw. A slight crook in his nose was all that saved him from perfection.

And his mouth…

She dipped the cloth into the water again and smoothed it over his dry, parched lips, moistening them. Hearing his low moan of gratitude, she found her mind straying again, this time to wonder what his lips would feel like pressed against hers. She was sure his kisses would be hard, demanding, seductive, much like the image he projected. Mesmerized by the shape of his mouth, his lips' texture, she stilled her hand at the bow of his upper lip and stared, all but able to taste the salty sweat that beaded the skin above it, feel the rasp of his day-old beard chafing against her skin.

Heat flooded her cheeks and pooled in her belly, as the image grew. She quickly plunged the cloth into the water again, determined to keep her mind focused on his wounds. Though it was difficult, she made herself finish cleansing his face, then plucked a gauze pad from the kit and soaked it with antiseptic.

"I'm going to put on the antiseptic now," she warned.

"Do it quick. That stuff burns like—"

Before he could say more, Maggie squeezed, drizzling the liquid over his cheek.

He sat bolt upright, his eyes flipping wide. "Holy sh—!" Groaning, he clamped an arm around his middle and sank weakly back against the chair.

Knowing how much pain that movement must have caused him, Maggie laid a sympathetic hand on his shoulder. "Sorry."

"Blow," he begged. "Please."

Without questioning the wisdom of that act, she leaned over and blew softly over the cut. His relief was almost immediate, evidenced by his sigh. She felt the moist warmth of it against her cheek, heard the low, throaty sound that accompanied it in the gust of air that wafted past her ear.

Sure that the stinging sensation had eased by now, she started to draw away, but he cuffed a hand at the back of her neck, stopping her.

"Again."

Though she knew it would be wiser to refuse, the husky plea in his voice, the desperate clasp of his fingers around her neck had her inhaling a deep breath. As she blew, his scent swirled around her, filled her. The musky, masculine odors of sweat, leather and horses tangled together, clouding her mind and forming a knot of keen awareness that settled low in her belly.

It would be so easy to kiss him right now, she thought. They were so close. A slight turn of the head…a pucker. Then she'd know what his kiss was like, his taste.

Even as the tempting thought formed in her mind, she felt his fingers tighten on her neck, sensed the tensing of his body. Mortified that he had somehow read her thoughts, she snapped her gaze to his and saw that his eyes were open and focused on her. In the blue depths she saw the same heat, the same question that burned behind hers.

His gaze slid to her mouth, and heat seared her chest, her cheeks, her throat, quickened her pulse. Unconsciously, she wet her lips, and he groaned, his eyes following the arc of her tongue. Slowly he raised his eyes to meet hers.

"You know what a mistake this would be."

She didn't need to ask what he meant by *this*. Gulping, she nodded. "Yes…I know."

With his gaze on hers, he drew her face to his. He touched his mouth to hers once, briefly, withdrew, and inhaled deeply, as if to savor the flavors he'd found there. Then, with a groan, he opened his mouth over hers and covered hers, capturing her lips, her very soul. The heat was instantaneous, blinding, debilitating. Closing her eyes against it, she braced her hands against his shoulders to keep from sinking weakly to her knees.

His kiss was everything she'd imagined it to be. Hard, demanding…yet gloriously seductive. His teeth nipped, his tongue soothed. Greedy, yet at the same time tender, captivating. She knew she should turn away or, at the very

least, put up a halfhearted struggle, but found she couldn't.
She wanted the kiss to go on and on and never end.

He cupped a hand at her hip. "Closer," he murmured,
as he urged her down to his lap.

She'd barely settled there, before he was pushing her hair
back over her shoulder to bury his face in the curve of her
neck.

"Better," he said, with a sigh, as he dragged his tongue
along the narrow channel above her collar bone.

Rocked by the sensations that flooded her, frightened by
them, she dug her fingers into his shoulders. "Ace," she
gasped. "You have to—"

Before she could tell him to stop, demand that he do so,
he brought his mouth back to hers, silencing her. With her
hips gripped between his hands, he slid down lower on the
chair and stretched out his long legs, shifting her around
until they were positioned chest-to-chest, groin-to-groin,
thigh-to-thigh. Holding her hard against him, he thrust his
tongue between her lips and stole her breath, along with
whatever power she had to stop him.

Gradually she became aware of his erection thickening
and lengthening between them. She could almost hear the
blood rushing into it, making it swell, feel the heat that
fired it, forging it into a thick shaft of steel between them.
An ache throbbed to life between her legs and she rolled
her hips over his erection, desperate to ease it. She heard
his low groan, felt the painful dig of his fingers into her
buttocks, and was sure he was suffering the same frustrations as she.

Dizzy with need, for a moment she felt as if she were
falling, but was sure she was only imagining the sensation.
A split second later her bottom struck the tile floor with
enough momentum to jar her teeth. Stunned, she blinked
open her eyes to find Ace standing over her, his arms vised
around his chest, his head flung back, his teeth bared.

Fury shot through her at him treating her so carelessly.

But it drained away just as quickly, when she realized the expression on his face was one of pain. Alarmed, she scrambled to her feet. "Oh, my God, Ace! Did you hurt your ribs?"

He dropped his chin to glare at her. "*I* didn't. *You* did."

She fell back a step. "Me?"

"Yes, you. With all that thrashing and grinding you were doing, if my ribs weren't busted before, they sure as hell are now."

Stunned, for a moment she could only stare. Then the anger came, filling her with a blinding rage.

"I wouldn't have been anywhere near your ribs, if you hadn't dragged me down onto your lap!"

"How the hell was I supposed to know that you were so starved for sex that you'd paw me half to death?"

Her mouth dropped open, then slammed shut with an indignant click of teeth. Taking a threatening step toward him. she stabbed a finger against the middle of his chest. "*You're* the desperate one. All I did was blow on your cut, just like you asked me to do. The rest was *your* doing."

He shoved her hand away. "And what the hell did you expect me to do, with you rubbing yourself all over me and blowing in my ear?"

"I was blowing on your cheek!"

"Same damn thing. You were—"

Cocking her head toward the hall, she threw up a hand to silence him and listened. Dropping her arm, she glared at him. "Now look what you've done."

"What?" he cried in frustration.

She spun on her heel and marched for the door. "You woke up the baby."

"Me!" he shouted after her. "You were yelling just as loud as I was!" When she didn't respond, he gave the chair an angry kick, then flopped down on it and glared at the empty doorway, his blood boiling at all the injustices that kept piling up on him.

First his old man up and dies, leaving him an estate to settle with no will to use as a guide and a ranch to manage with no ranch hands to do the work. If that wasn't bad enough, he then gets stuck with a baby he doesn't want and winds up hiring the nanny from hell to take care of the kid.

She didn't ask for the job, a small voice reminded him. *You all but bulldozed her into taking it on. And, she was right about you starting all this. You were the one who pulled her down on your lap.*

Ace squirmed uncomfortably at his conscience's prodding.

Okay, he admitted reluctantly. So maybe he was partially to blame for what had happened. But what man wouldn't have reacted the same as he had, if caught in a similar situation? Having a woman rubbing her hands all over you and blowing her hot breath in your ear, when you'd spent the last six months alone on a photo shoot in the remote mountains of Central America, where the closest you'd come to female companionship was an overly friendly donkey, who stole your food out of your backpack? Hell, it was a wonder he hadn't thrown Maggie down on the floor and taken her right then and there!

But sex complicated things. Always did. Ace knew that. And he sure as hell wasn't going to take a chance on getting physically involved with Maggie. He needed her to take care of the kid a lot worse than he needed an outlet for his sexual frustrations.

Exhausted from the lack of sleep he'd gotten the night before, as well as the long, hot trek back to the house, he leaned his head back with a sigh and closed his eyes, vowing a life of celibacy.

At least where Maggie was concerned.

Four

Ace wasn't sure how much time had passed before he heard Maggie's footsteps, signaling her return. Minutes? Hours? Could've been either, because he'd lost all sense of time the second he'd closed his eyes.

Too tired to rouse himself, he asked groggily, "Was the kid okay?"

"She was fine."

He felt something soft brush his chest, a strange warmth, followed by the scent of talcum powder. Opening his eyes, he looked down to find the baby on his chest and Maggie guiding his hand to the infant's back.

He tried to wrench his hand free. "What do you think you're doing? I'm not holding this kid!"

"I can't very well hold her and wrap your ribs, too."

He narrowed an eye at her. "Like I'm gonna let you anywhere near my ribs."

Folding her arms across her chest, she looked down her

nose at him. "So you've changed your mind about going to see a doctor?"

"I'm not going anywhere. Now get this kid off me."

She plucked a roll of elastic bandage from the first aid kit. "I will as soon as I've wrapped your ribs."

"But she's naked!"

"Oh, she is not," Maggie fussed. "She has a diaper on. I just took her gown off, so she could air out for awhile."

"Well, let her air out someplace else."

She looked around the room. "And where would you suggest I put her? In the refrigerator?" Frowning, she shook her head. "No, it's too full. She'd never fit. How about the sink?"

"Very funny."

"I'm not trying to be funny. I'm *trying* to make you see that there's no place else to put her but on your lap. You really should buy one of those infant swings. She'd like that. Tell me if this hurts," she said, and pressed her fingers lightly against his ribs.

Her touch, though light, sent pain lancing through his side. Ace would have jumped up and howled like a wounded dog, if he hadn't been afraid he'd drop the kid.

He curled his lip in a snarl. "First thing tomorrow morning I want you to go to town and buy a damn swing and whatever else this kid needs."

She fluttered her eyelashes at him. "How could I possibly refuse, with you asking so sweetly?" Losing the fake smile, she waved an impatient hand. "Now hold her out of the way, so that I can bandage your chest."

When he didn't make a move to comply, she huffed a breath, plucked his hand from the baby's back and picked the baby up herself. Unable to resist, she took a moment to nuzzle Laura's cheek before draping a blanket over Ace's legs and laying the infant, stomach down, across his thighs.

She reached for his hand again, but he snatched it away.

"I know the drill," he growled, and spread his fingers over the baby's back, holding her in place.

With a shrug, Maggie picked up the roll of elastic bandage and placed an end in the middle of Ace's chest. "Lean forward a little," she instructed, as she moved to his side and began wrapping the tape around him.

When she'd finished, she stepped back to admire her work. "Not bad, even if I do say so myself."

"Great. Now would you please get this kid off me?"

She held up a finger. "Just give me a second to put these things away."

She quickly gathered the first aid supplies and put them back into the kit, then turned for the mudroom to return it to the chest. As she did, she shrieked and jumped back, knocking against Ace's shoulder.

"What the hell's the matter with you?" he shouted. "You almost made me drop the kid."

"There's a man—"

Before she could tell him there was a man outside the door, peering through the glass, the man in question opened the door and stepped inside.

"Did I scare you?" he asked Maggie, but was grinning as if he knew he had and thought her reaction funny.

Ace's back was to the door, making it impossible for him to see their visitor, but he must have recognized the voice.

"A face like that would scare the hell out of anybody," he grumbled.

Tossing his hat onto the counter, the stranger crossed to Maggie, his hand extended in greeting. "Rory Tanner, ma'am." He tipped his head toward Ace. "I'm this old cuss's younger and much more handsome brother."

Up close, Maggie could see the resemblance between the two, though Rory was leaner than Ace and seemed to have been blessed with a much more pleasant disposition. Releasing the breath she'd been holding, she accepted his hand. ''Maggie Dean. I'm Laura's nanny.''

When she tried to withdraw her hand, Rory held on. Smiling, he drew her hand to his lips and brushed a kiss over her knuckles. ''Ace told me that he'd hired someone, but he failed to mention how pretty you are.''

''Oh, for crying out loud,'' Ace groused. ''Quit your flirting, Rory, and get over here and get this kid.''

Shooting her a wink, Rory gave her hand a parting squeeze, then moved in front of Ace. His eyes widened in surprise, when he got his first look at his brother. ''Whoa. What truck ran over you?''

Ace averted his gaze, obviously embarrassed to admit how he'd received the injuries. ''Dang horse pitched me off.''

''I told him he should see a doctor,'' Maggie said, ''but he refused.''

Rory shook his head. ''That's no surprise. Ace has a powerful fear of doctors.''

''I do not!'' Ace cried.

''I stand corrected,'' Rory said, bowing. ''It's their *needles* that scare you.'' Chuckling, he glanced over at Maggie. ''One time, when we were kids, I stepped on a rusty nail and Ace had to take me to the doctor to get a tetanus shot. Even insisted upon holding my hand while they gave me the injection. One look at that needle, and he passed smooth out. Took two nurses to revive him.''

''Shoulda let you die from blood poisoning or lockjaw,'' Ace grumbled, then snapped, ''If you don't take this kid, I'm dumping her on the floor.''

Maggie quickly stepped between the two men, fearing Ace would make good his threat.

''Here, I'll take her.'' She lifted the baby to her shoulder, then offered Ace a hand. ''Need some help?''

He slapped her hand away. "It's my ribs that're hurt, not my legs."

But when he tried to stand, his butt only cleared the chair about three inches before he was sinking back down, his face pale, his hand clasped at his side.

Rory moved closer. "Here, Ace. I'll help you."

Ace shot him a murderous look. "I don't need your help. What I need is whiskey. See if there's any in the liquor cabinet in the den."

Rory turned away, biting back a smile. "Sure thing, Ace. Won't take me but a minute."

"If you're in pain," Maggie said worriedly, "I'll get you some aspirin."

"I don't want aspirin. I want whiskey."

"But, Ace—"

"And make it straight," he shouted to Rory.

Rory returned with a bottle and a glass. He splashed two fingers of whiskey into the tumbler, then offered it to Ace. Ace looked pointedly at the glass, then up at Rory. With a shrug, Rory filled it to the top and passed it to Ace.

Ace downed half the drink in one greedy gulp, shuddered, then sank back in the chair with a sigh. "I feel better already."

Rory set the whiskey bottle on the table. "Another shot like that, and you won't feel anything at all."

Maggie pushed the bottle out of Ace's reach. "What you need is food, not whiskey."

"Food?" Rory echoed, his eyes lighting up. "Is there any of Mrs. Frazier's fried chicken left?"

"If there isn't," Maggie told him, "there's plenty more to choose from. If you'll hold the baby, I'll see what I can find."

Rory took a step back, rubbing his hands down the side of his legs. "I don't think so. I've never held a kid before."

Maggie rolled her eyes. "What is it with you Tanner men? She won't bite."

"No, but she might break."

"Oh, for heaven's sake," Maggie fussed, then dragged out a chair and pointed a stiff finger at it. "Sit," she ordered.

Rory sat.

"You'll have to support her head," she warned him. "She's not strong enough yet to hold it up on her own."

He blew out an uneasy breath, wiped his palms down his thighs, then held out his arms. "Okay. Hand her over."

She transferred the baby into his arms, tucking the blanket carefully around her. "There," she said, smiling as she straightened. "That's not so hard, is it?"

Rory looked down at the baby, who was staring up at him in wide-eyed wonder, and grinned. "She's a cute little thing, isn't she?"

"Precious," Ace muttered under his breath, then said louder, "Is anybody going to pour me another drink or am I going to have to get up and get it myself?"

When Rory and Maggie ignored him, Ace set his jaw and dug in his heels, scooching his chair closer to the table. Slamming the empty glass down on its top, he grabbed the bottle and turned it up, gulping whiskey as fast as he could swallow. The liquid burned a path down his throat and hit his empty stomach with a nauseating splash.

Sure that Maggie would have stopped him by now—or at the very least have voiced her disapproval—he lowered the bottle and stole a glance her way. She stood at Rory's side, her arm draped along the back of his chair, her face almost cheek-to-cheek with his, smiling and offering encouragement, as Rory fed the baby the bottle.

For some stupid reason, seeing the two together like that made Ace madder than hell.

"I thought you were going to fix us something to eat?" he snapped.

Maggie leaned to place her hand over Rory's to adjust the angle of the bottle. "I am," she said, as she straightened. "I just wanted to make sure Rory was comfortable with feeding Laura first." She smiled at Rory and gave him a pat on the back. "You're doing great," she said, before turning away.

Ace watched her cross to the refrigerator, a scowl building on his face.

"I don't know what he's doing that's so great," he grumbled. "Any fool can feed a baby."

Maggie pulled open the refrigerator door, then looked over the top of it at Ace. "You ought to know," she said, smiling sweetly. "You managed to do it."

Ace awakened slowly, sure that a woodpecker had set up shop on his forehead and was jackhammering a hole between his eyes. Moaning, he rolled to his back, then sucked in a breath through his teeth, as pain stabbed through his side. Remembering his fall from the horse, he closed his eyes and gulped, willing the nausea back.

When he was fairly certain he could do so without throwing up, he opened his eyes and looked around. Since his last memory was of sitting at the kitchen table, guzzling whiskey straight from the bottle, he was surprised to find himself in his bed and in his room. How had he gotten there? he wondered. Maggie? Rory?

Neither, he decided, scowling. If left up to the two of them, he could've died in that chair and they wouldn't have noticed. They'd been too busy flirting with each other to care what happened to him. Rory he could almost understand, since his brother was a natural born flirt. But Maggie? Hadn't she professed to Ace, only that morning, that she wasn't interested in a relationship with a man, sexual or otherwise?

Hard to believe, after that hot little tango she'd danced with Ace in the kitchen, prior to Rory's arrival. His scowl deepened. Harder still, considering the way she'd latched onto Rory like he was the last living male on earth, preparing him a plate of food and all but hand feeding it to him, while he gave the baby the bottle.

And what had Maggie done for Ace, who was too busted up to stand alone, much less get himself something to eat? Nothing but shoot him dirty looks every time he lifted the bottle for another drink.

You wouldn't be jealous now would you, Tanner?

The question came out of nowhere and had Ace stiffening. Hell, no, he wasn't jealous, he told himself, forcing the tension from his shoulders. He didn't give a tinker's damn if Maggie had the hots for his brother. Why should he care who she fooled around with, as long as she stayed away from him and kept the kid out of his hair?

The bedroom door opened a crack, and he whipped his head around just as Maggie's face appeared in the opening. She looked a little bit too pink-cheeked and cheerful to suit Ace.

"What do you want?" he snapped.

Her smile dipping into a frown, she pushed the door open and stepped inside. "Well, I see that a good night's sleep hasn't improved your disposition any."

Remembering that he was wearing nothing but his boxer shorts, he yanked the sheet across his lower body. "Nothing wrong with my disposition."

Arching a brow, she crossed to the bed. "So you're always this cranky?"

Before he could think of a suitable comeback, she distracted him by leaning to fluff the pillows behind his head. With her body draped across his, he got a whiff of some come-hither perfume and a peek of cleavage that kicked his senses into overload and his hormones into high gear. Down, boy, he told himself, remembering his vow of celibacy where she was concerned.

Straightening, she gave him a stern look. "You owe Rory a big thank-you."

He snorted a disgusted breath. "For what? Feeding the baby her damn bottle?"

"No. For taking you to the emergency room."

He gaped at her. "He didn't take me anywhere."

She smiled smugly. "Oh, but he did. That's just one of the consequences of consuming too much alcohol. It robs a person of whole blocks of time."

Groaning, Ace squeezed a hand at his temples, unable to believe he'd been so drunk he didn't remember a trip to the emergency room.

"By the way," she added. "You'll be glad to know that your ribs aren't broken, just bruised."

"Which is what I said all along," he snapped.

Ignoring him, she went on. "And while you're thanking Rory, you might want to throw in an apology."

"An apology?" he cried. "For *what?*"

"You called him a few choice names, while he was helping you to bed."

Though he was relieved to learn that it was Rory and not Maggie who had stripped him of his clothes, Ace wasn't about to offer his brother an apology. He folded his arms stubbornly across his chest. "Probably deserved it."

"What he *deserves* is an apology."

He eyed her suspiciously, wondering why she was so hell-bent on defending Rory and wondering, too, if it was his brother who had put that pretty shade of pink in her cheeks and left her looking as satisfied as a cat with a belly full of cream. "What time did he leave, anyway?"

She shrugged. "I don't know. Ten or eleven, I'd guess."

"How long before that did he put me to bed?"

"He left right after." She gave him an odd look. "Why?"

Jutting his chin, he looked away. "No reason."

With a shrug, she leaned to press the back of her fingers against his forehead.

He ducked away. "What the hell do you think you're doing?"

"Checking to see if you have a temperature."

"What I have is a headache."

She stooped to pick his clothes up from the floor. "And well earned. You drank enough whiskey to kill a normal person."

He would've argued, but since he felt a little like death, he decided against it. "Get me some aspirin."

She dumped his clothes on the foot of his bed to fist her hands on her hips. "Oh, so you want aspirin now? When I offered them to you last night, all you wanted was whiskey."

His stomach churned sickly at the reminder of the bottle he'd polished off. Or was it two? "Aspirin," he repeated.

With a huff of breath, she dropped her hands from her hips and marched to the adjoining bath. She returned minutes later with a bottle and a glass of water. She shook a couple of tablets onto his palm, then passed him the water to wash them down with.

"Your agent called," she told him while he drank. "He wants you to call him. He said it was an emergency."

Ace backhanded the water from his upper lip. "Everything's an emergency to Max."

She took the glass from him and set it on the bedside table. "He said something about your book being short and your publisher needing more photographs before they can send it on to the printer."

Ace sat bolt upright at the news, then sank weakly back

against the pillows, holding a hand against his bandaged ribs. "What next?" he moaned miserably.

"Do you want me to call him and tell him that you had an accident and can't take care of any business right now?"

"No, I don't want you to tell him any such thing!" He frowned a moment, thinking. "There's a portfolio in the back seat of my truck." He held his hands out, measuring. "About this size and black. Bring it to me."

She lifted a brow. "You might try asking a little nicer."

He set his jaw, knowing she had him between a rock and a hard place, since he wasn't at all sure he could make it to his truck under his own steam. "Please," he ground out between clenched teeth.

She smiled. "All right. But I'll need to check on the baby first. Do you want anything else?"

A break from bad news, Ace thought irritably, but shook his head. "Just the portfolio."

Later that morning, Ace sat propped up in his bed, studying the prints spread in front of him, trying to decide if he could use any for the book. Busted up like he was, making another trip to Wyoming to take additional shots was out of the question.

"Ace?"

He looked up to find Maggie standing in the doorway, the baby in her arms. "What?"

"I'm going to town to buy some supplies for Laura. How do you want me to pay for them?"

He turned his attention back to the photos. "Charge whatever you need. The Bar-T has accounts at every store in town."

"Do you want me to bring you something to eat before I leave? You haven't eaten anything this morning."

Ace's stomach growled at the reminder. "I suppose I could choke down something."

She stepped into the room and crossed to the bed. "I found a lemon pound cake in the refrigerator and there's fresh coffee brewed. How does that sound?"

Without looking up, he waved her away. "Whatever."

He heard a rustling sound and glanced over to find Maggie had moved some of his photos aside and was laying the baby on the bed beside him. "You're not leaving that kid here!" he cried.

"It's just for a minute," she promised, as she hurried for the door. "I can't carry her and a tray, too."

"Wait! I—" Before he could tell Maggie he'd changed his mind about being hungry, she was gone. Scowling down at the baby, he snatched a photo from beneath her foot. "Don't touch a thing," he warned.

She blinked up at him, as if fascinated by the sound of his voice. Curling his lip in disgust, he turned his attention back to his work, determined to ignore the kid.

But a few seconds later, he found his gaze straying back to her.

She is kind of cute, he thought, remembering Rory's comment the night before. But, damn, she was tiny. He touched the tip of his finger against a palm no bigger than a quarter and nearly jumped out of his skin, when she closed her fingers around his. His heart thumping wildly, he tried to pull his finger from her grasp, but she held on tight.

"That's quite a grip you've got there, kid," he said uneasily. Though he wasn't certain, he would swear the little gurgling sound she made was a laugh. He narrowed an eye at her. "So you think this is funny, do you?" He shook his finger, trying to break her grip. His eyes widened in amazement, when he couldn't shake loose. "What are you? Wonder Kid?"

In answer, she lifted her legs and planted her bare feet

against his forearm. He stared at them, astonished at how small they were, how soft.

"If you plan on doing any walking on those things," he told her, "you'd better do some growing."

"She'll grow."

Ace glanced up to find Maggie entering the room, a tray in her hands. Embarrassed that she'd caught him talking to the kid, he jerked his hand back and was relieved the kid chose that moment to release her hold on him.

"She'd better," he grumbled.

Maggie shifted items on the bedside table, making room for the tray. "I wasn't sure what you'd want in your coffee, so I brought both cream and sugar."

Ace reached for the cup and drew it to his lips, all but salivating at the coffee's rich aroma. "Black's fine," he said, before gulping down a swallow. Closing his eyes, he sank back against the pillows with a sigh. "Is there any way you can rig this up to my arm and feed it to me intravenously?"

In spite of her irritation with him, Maggie had to resist a smile at the desperation in his voice. "I don't think so."

While he sipped his coffee, she glanced at the photos spread over the bed. Her curiosity aroused by the black and white shots, she picked one of the photos up to examine it more closely. Captured on the print was a moose, with only its head and antlers visible, peeking around the corner of a weathered barn.

"This is good," she said, impressed by Ace's skill with a camera. "Is this one of the pictures you've chosen to send to your agent?"

He set aside his coffee and took the photo from her. "Maybe," he said, studying it critically. "I haven't decided yet."

Maggie sat down on the side of the bed, absently stroking her fingers up and down the baby's arm, as she looked over the other photos. "What's your book about?" she asked curiously.

"Wyoming." He laid the photo aside and picked up another. "Specifically, the wildlife and domesticized animals found there." He angled the photo he held for her to see. "What do you think of this one?"

The photo was of a little boy and his dog, both dripping wet from a swim in the lake behind them. Charmed by the expressions on the faces of the two, she said the first thought that came to mind. "Best friends."

Ace's eyes sharpened at her response. "Exactly," he said, then tossed the picture aside to pick up another. "And this one?"

Her smile melted as she stared at the picture of an emaciated dog, its ribs protruding grotesquely, digging through a garbage can. In the near distance, a man was pulling a gun from the backseat of his truck. Gulping, she looked up at Ace. "He didn't shoot the dog, did he?"

Ace was too interested in her responses to take time to respond. Dropping the photo, he picked up another to hold before her face. "What about this one?"

Maggie shoved his hand aside. "Please tell me that you didn't let him shoot the dog."

"The dog's fine," he said in frustration, then pushed the photo back in front of her eyes. "What do you see?"

Giving him a doubtful look, Maggie shifted her gaze to the picture and a tender smile curved her lips. "A mother's love."

"That's all?"

She looked up at him, her forehead creasing in puzzlement. "Yes. What was I supposed to see?"

Ace turned the picture around to frown at it. He'd slipped up on the doe in a secluded glen at daybreak, catching the deer lying on a bed of crushed grass, her fawn asleep at her side. He'd snapped the picture just as the doe had turned her head to lick the fawn's face. To him the picture represented peace, tranquility. Nature at its best.

But Maggie had seen only a mother's love.

With a shrug, he set the picture aside. "You put the kid to sleep with all that petting."

Maggie glanced down and was surprised to see that Laura had, indeed, fallen asleep. Smiling, she scooped the infant into her arms and rose. "I guess I better head for town while she's napping."

He dropped his gaze to the photos again, searching for a common thread that would link them together. "Charge whatever you need."

"Do you want me to pick up anything for you while I'm in town?"

He shifted the order of the photos, removed two, then studied them critically. "I need to ship these off to my agent."

"No problem. I can do it for you while I'm in town. I'll need the address."

Seeing the thread he needed, he plucked another picture out of the line-up and tossed it aside, then quickly began gathering the remaining photos and slipping them into protective sleeves. "Never mind. I'll go with you."

Maggie looked at him in surprise. "But your ribs," she reminded him.

He shot her a scowl. "They're only bruised, remember?" He started to whip the sheet back to rise, but caught himself. Holding the sheet at his waist in a fist, he lifted a brow. "Not that I have anything I'd be ashamed for you to see, but you might want to wait outside."

Five

The downtown area of Tanner Crossing was built on the town square concept, with Tanner State Bank sitting dead center. An eclectic mix of retail shops and business offices lined the four streets forming the square, each building's front unique in design and ornamentation, yet blending to create a charming retail center enticing enough to satisfy the shopping needs of visitors and locals alike.

Pushing the newly-purchased stroller down the awning-shaded sidewalk, Maggie glanced wistfully at the window displays she passed, wishing she had time to browse through some of the shops. But Ace's instructions had been specific. One hour, he'd said, and she was to meet him back at the truck. He'd even added the warning that if she was late, he was leaving without her.

Maggie didn't doubt for a minute that he would make good his threat. He was just that ornery.

Fortunately, she'd found most of the things she needed

in the first store she'd stopped at. In less than thirty minutes, she'd purchased a crib, a swing and the stroller, plus filled three huge shopping bags with an assortment of other baby items. But she could never have accomplished so much so quickly if not for the Tanner name. It had barely slipped past her lips, when the owner himself had appeared and had his sales staff all but turning the store inside out in his anxiousness to fill her requests. He'd even agreed to deliver all her purchases to the ranch later in the week at no extra charge.

Still shaking her head over what a difference a name could make, Maggie pushed open the door to the drugstore and carefully maneuvered the stroller over the threshold. Once inside, she stopped to get her bearings and had to blink twice, sure that she'd been catapulted back in time to the '50s. An old-fashioned soda fountain, complete with chrome pedestaled bar stools bolted to a black-and-white tiled floor, dominated the wall on her left. The opposite side of the store held the beauty counter, with cosmetics and perfumes displayed on gleaming glass shelves, and feminine products wrapped in plain brown paper. In between stretched aisle after aisle of merchandise-laden shelving units, the products on each ranging from greeting cards to hand-held massagers. At the rear of the store hung a red neon ℞ guiding customers back to the pharmacy, where a gray-haired man stood on a tall ladder, stocking the shelves with a new shipment of medications.

With a quick glance at her watch to check the time, Maggie pushed the stroller down the aisle marked Infant Care. She quickly selected the toiletries and diapers she needed, placed them on the rack beneath the stroller, then moved on to study the selections of formula and baby food.

"Can I help you find something?"

Maggie glanced over to find a woman bustling down the aisle toward her. Wearing a pastel smock with Samples'

Pharmacy embroidered over the left breast, she moved with a speed that belied her plumpness and snow-white hair.

Maggie offered her a hopeful smile. "You can if you know when it's safe to start a baby on fruits and cereals."

"Safe?" the woman repeated, then huffed a breath. "Honey, you've been reading too many of those new mother books." She gave Maggie's arm a patronizing pat. "But most young folks do with their first."

Before Maggie could explain that Laura wasn't her baby, the woman thrust out her hand.

"I'm Myrna Samples. My husband, John, is the pharmacist." As Maggie took the woman's hand, Myrna leaned close to whisper, "But don't let that fancy title of his fool you. He may know all there is to know about all those little pills that he guards like the national mint, but I'm the authority on babies." She swelled her chest proudly. "Raised four of my own, plus helped raise twelve grandchildren and five greats."

Laughing, Maggie inclined her head. "I bow to your greater experience. I'm Maggie," she said, then gestured to the baby. "And this is Laura."

Myrna stooped to peer beneath the stroller's umbrella at the baby. "Oh, but she's a pretty little thing," she said, then looked up at Maggie. "How old is she?"

"Almost four weeks."

Myrna straightened, her arthritic knees creaking at the effort. "Is she sleeping through the night?"

"No. She usually wakes up between one and two, wanting a bottle."

Myrna pulled a box from the shelf. "Then, you'll want to put a little cereal in her formula. Rice is best, until you've determined if she has any food allergies."

Maggie took the box and added it to the other items beneath the stroller. "Thanks," she said gratefully. "Her formula wasn't seeming to satisfy her any more, but I wasn't sure if I should introduce a new food into her diet this soon, without talking to a doctor first.''

"Go with the gut,'' Myrna said prosaically. "That's what I always say. A mother knows best what her child needs.''

Again, Maggie tried to explain that she wasn't Laura's mother, but Myrna interrupted her by asking, '' Are you needing anything else?''

Maggie glanced at her list. "No. That about does it.''

"Then follow me,'' Myrna said and led the way to the checkout. She helped remove the items from beneath the stroller, then stepped behind the cash register and rang up the purchases. "Cash or charge?'' she asked, when she'd finished.

"Charge,'' Maggie replied, then added, "To the Bar-T.''

Frowning, Myrna dipped her chin to look at Maggie over the top of her reading glasses. "The Bar-T?''

Maggie felt a moment's unease. "Well…yes. The Tanners do have an account here, don't they? Ace said I was to charge whatever I needed.''

Myrna's brows shot high. "That sweet child is Ace Tanner's?''

Heat flooded Maggie's cheeks. "Well, no,'' she said hesitantly, unsure if Ace would want the whole town to know about Laura's existence. "Not exactly. Ace is Laura's…guardian.''

Myrna stared at Maggie a moment, then sputtered a laugh. "Well, I suppose that's one way of explaining their relationship.'' She hit a register key and a receipt churned out. Tearing it off, she laid it on the counter. "Sign right here,'' she said, then leaned a hip against the counter and folded her arms over her ample breasts. "And here I was thinking that Ace had quit cleaning up after his daddy years ago,'' she said, with a regretful shake of her head.

Maggie passed her the receipt. "Excuse me?''

Myrna flapped a hand, as she tucked the slip of paper into a slot on the register drawer. "Not that I blame Ace, you understand. Buck was nothing but a rounder, and a selfish one at that. Left the raising of his sons up to that poor wife of his. After the cancer got Emma, the old coot didn't show a sign of changing his ways, so Ace stepped in and took over the job." She shook her head sadly. "Poor thing. Wasn't much more than a boy himself, at the time."

While Maggie stared, trying her best to hide her shock, Myrna began to chuckle.

"You should have seen those boys when Ace brought them to town. They'd trail along behind him like a gaggle of baby geese after a mother goose. As they got older, I think they began to resent him bossin' them around. Especially Ry," she added with a frown, then sighed. "But I guess that was to be expected, as he was the closest to Ace in age. But Ace never once backed off from the responsibility he'd taken on, no matter how big a fuss those boys kicked up." She shook her head. "No, siree, he stuck by those brothers of his through thick and thin."

Rearing back, she flapped a hand. "Would you listen to me? Here I am talking your ear off, when I'm sure you've got other errands to run."

Caught up in the glimpse of Ace's past Myrna had woven for her, Maggie had forgotten all about the time. She glanced at her wrist watch and was surprised to see that her hour was almost up. "I really do need to go," she said, panicking. "I'm supposed to meet Ace back at the truck soon. Thanks again for your help, Myrna."

"Anytime, honey," Myrna called after her. "And you be sure and bring that sweet baby back by to see me the next time you're in town, you hear?"

"I will," Maggie promised.

Praying Ace hadn't arrived yet, Maggie all but flew across the street to the spot where she was to meet him.

Not seeing a sign of him anywhere, she heaved a sigh of relief and slowed, pushing the stroller to a park bench beneath the shade of a centuries-old oak tree. Sitting down to wait, she rolled the stroller slowly back and forth, gently rocking the baby, and thought back over her conversation with Myrna.

She tried to picture Ace as a young boy, as Myrna had described him, traipsing through town, with his three brothers in tow. Though the image came easily enough to mind, she couldn't begin to imagine what it must have been like for a boy his age to take on the responsibilities of caring for his three younger brothers—especially after they reached an age where they resented his supervision.

She might have been able to dismiss Myrna's comments as an old woman's rambling, if she hadn't remembered Rory telling her the night before about Ace taking him to the doctor to get a tetanus shot. At the time, Maggie hadn't thought much about the story, other than thinking it was funny that a man as tough as Ace was terrified of needles. But now she realized what a courageous and selfless act that had been for Ace. With no parent around to handle the emergency, he'd set aside his own fears and taken Rory to the doctor, even insisting upon holding his brother's hand while Rory was given the dreaded shot.

Kind. Giving. Compassionate. They were all adjectives that fit the picture of the young Ace Myrna and Rory had drawn for her. But Maggie had a hard time associating those traits with the adult version of that boy.

But maybe that was partly her fault, she thought, trying to be fair. She'd been so blinded by her own grief and so determined that the Tanners should raise Laura, that she'd never once considered Ace's feelings before she'd thrust the baby on him.

In retrospect, she could see why he hadn't exactly welcomed Laura with open arms. In a matter of only a few days, he'd lost his father, assumed the duties of executor of what must be a sizeable and complicated estate and had the guardianship of a half sister, whom he hadn't even known existed, all but dumped on his lap. A lot for any man to deal with, she thought, feeling a stab of remorse for the lack of understanding and compassion she'd offered him.

The sound of approaching footsteps jarred her from her thoughts, and she glanced up to find Ace coming down the sidewalk toward her. He walked with his head down, his hands shoved deeply into his pockets and his shoulders stooped, as if he carried the weight of the world on them.

Emotion tightened her throat. She wanted to believe that it was his slight limp and battered appearance that caused the unexpected swell of emotion. But it was something more than his injuries that had her curling her hands around the edge of the bench to keep herself from jumping up and running to meet him. Something stronger and decidedly scarier that had her wanting to throw herself into his arms.

And that something felt a whole lot like desire.

It was because he'd kissed her, she told herself, even now able to feel the warmth of his hands on her flesh, the smothering, yet captivating heat of his mouth covering hers. He'd made her feel things she'd never felt with a man before. Want things that she hadn't allowed herself to want in years. The memory of that kiss alone was enough to send her heart racing, but seeing him in the flesh made her yearn to experience the thrill of it all again.

Fearing she would give in to the temptation, she gripped her hands tighter on the edge of the bench's seat. *Laura,* she reminded herself sternly. She had to keep her mind focused on Laura and her purpose for being in Ace's home. She couldn't afford to let anything or anyone—especially Ace Tanner—distract her from her goal. Not when she wanted so desperately to convince the Tanners to keep the baby and raise her as their own.

She drew in a deep, steadying breath, then slowly exhaled. But it wouldn't hurt her to be kinder to him, she told herself. More understanding.

Promising herself that she could offer him both, without jeopardizing Laura's future, she forced a smile and rose to greet him. "Did you get all of your errands run?"

He strode right past her, without so much as a glance her way.

She stared after him, her eyes rounded in astonishment. How rude! she thought, her temper flaring at the obvious snub. She knew he'd heard her. How could he *not,* when he'd passed within feet of where she stood?

Setting her jaw, she pushed the stroller to the truck, where he already sat behind the wheel. When she reached for the door, he leaned across the seat and shoved it open, bumping it against her knee.

"Get in," he snapped.

A scathing retort leaped to Maggie's tongue, but she quickly swallowed it, remembering her vow to be more understanding.

Stooping to transfer the baby from the stroller to the car seat, she muttered under her breath, "If I don't kill him first."

Maggie rode in tight-lipped silence for about five miles before she dared open her mouth, without fear of biting Ace's head off. She probably wouldn't have spoken to him then, if she hadn't noticed that he had the truck headed in the opposite direction of the ranch.

"Where are we going?" she asked, trying to keep the resentment from her voice.

"Your house."

She whipped her head around to look at him. "My house? Why?"

"I need to look through Star's personal belongings." He glanced her way. "You do have her stuff, right?"

Squeezing her hands between her thighs, Maggie turned to face the windshield again, the thought of opening up those boxes making her sick to her stomach. "What little she had," she said uneasily, then stole a glance his way. "Why do you need her things?"

"I hired a private detective and he says things'll go quicker, if has something more than a name to go on. I'm hoping to find that something in her stuff."

Maggie tried to remember what she and Dixie had packed into the boxes, when they'd cleaned out Star's apartment. But she'd been so upset by Star's death, she really hadn't paid that much attention.

"There's not much," she said hesitantly. "Clothes. Shoes. A few personal items."

"What about a checkbook or canceled checks?"

She shook her head. "Star didn't have a bank account. She lived on a cash basis and pretty much from paycheck to paycheck."

"There has to be something," he said in frustration.

Though Maggie doubted he would find anything that would offer him a clue to Star's past, she kept her suspicions to herself and rode in silence, that knot of dread in her stomach winding tighter and tighter with each passing mile.

When he pulled to a stop in front of her house, she had to force herself to open the door and climb out. Reaching into the back seat to unfasten the car seat, she hitched it on her hip and led the way to the front door. She passed her house key to Ace, waited while he unlocked the door, then followed him inside. She'd barely made it across the threshold, when he skidded to a stop and she bumped into his back.

"Damn!" he swore, fanning the air in front of his face. "It's like an oven in here."

She quickly set the car seat on the sofa. "Sorry," she murmured and began opening windows. "I don't have air conditioning."

He dragged a sleeve across the perspiration already beading on his forehead. "Are you *that* hard up for money?"

Maggie had to bite her tongue to keep from telling him he ought to try poverty for awhile. Instead, she forced a smile and said, "A penny saved is a penny earned."

He shot her a dark look. "Let's get this over with and get out of here, before we both melt."

As anxious as he to leave, Maggie retrieved a box from her room, set it on the floor in front of him, then left to fetch another.

By the time she returned with the second box, Ace had ripped the tape off the first and was dumping its contents onto the floor. Sinking to her knees opposite him, Maggie sniffed back tears as she watched him sort through the meager pile of Star's possessions.

At the sound, Ace looked up at her. His hand stilled. "What's wrong with you?" he asked impatiently.

She shook her head, her eyes filling. "It's just so sad."

"What is?"

"This," she said, gesturing to the articles of clothing he'd dumped onto the floor. "Twenty-two years, and this is all Star had to show for her life."

Frowning, Ace drew his hands back and rubbed them up and down his thighs, suddenly feeling like a grave-robber. He didn't want to think about the woman who'd owned these things or what her life had been like. And he sure as hell didn't want to think about the part his father had played in that life or what difference he might have made if he'd assumed a more active role.

Setting his jaw, he started stuffing the clothes back into the box. "Possessions don't mean anything. Not in the final count. It's what a person does with his or her life that matters."

"I don't know that Star did anything with her life," Maggie said sadly, "other than give birth to Laura." She glanced toward the sofa, where the baby slept peacefully in the car seat. "But surely that must count for something."

Ace looked over at the baby, then away just as quickly, his frown deepening. "Last I heard, they weren't handing out awards to single women for getting themselves knocked up."

Maggie sank back on her heels to stare at him in horror. "I can't believe you said that!"

He lifted a shoulder. "It's the truth."

"Whether it is or not," she said furiously, "isn't the point. It was cruel and totally uncalled for. When your father refused to marry her, Star could have taken the easy way out and had an abortion. But she chose to keep her baby. I'd think that says a lot for her moral character."

"If she had any morals, she wouldn't have gotten pregnant in the first place."

Incensed, Maggie balled her hands into fists on her knees. "Oh, that is so like a man! Your entire gender is nothing but a bunch of lying cowards. You all go around telling women you love them and promising them the moon and the stars just to get them into bed with you. Then, when the woman winds up pregnant, you turn tail and run, leaving her to deal with the problem alone."

Ace slammed the lid down on the box and faced her. "Not *all* men. I, for one, have never lied to a woman to get her to go to bed with me, and I've never gotten one pregnant, either."

"Yet," she said, pointedly. "And if you ever did get a woman pregnant, I'd hope, for the child's sake, that you *would* turn tail and run."

"And why would you want me to do that?"

"No child deserves a father who's incapable of loving or caring for them."

"Who says I'm incapable of caring for a kid?"

Lifting a brow, Maggie tipped her head toward the sofa and the baby sleeping in the car seat.

Ace scowled. "She's not my kid."

"No. She's your sister."

"Half sister," he corrected.

"And being only 'half' prevents you from loving her or caring what happens to her?"

"Aren't I trying my damnedest to find Star's relatives so that the kid will have a home?"

"You're trying to get rid of her," Maggie told him. "And what happens to Laura if you don't find a relative?"

He opened his mouth, then clamped it shut again. Grabbing the second box, he ripped the top open and dumped its contents on the floor. Confronted with nothing but more clothes and a tangle of shoes, he lurched to his feet. "This is nothing but a waste of time."

As he strode for the door, Maggie stared after him, wincing when he slammed it behind him. Slowly she began to gather the scattered clothes and shoes.

Well, so much for kindness and understanding, she thought glumly.

Maggie stepped back to admire her work, pleased with the way the nursery had turned out. Though she'd deliberated long and hard over how far to go with the room's transformation, she'd finally decided it best to keep Laura's integration into the Tanner household as unobtrusive and subtle as possible. As a result, she'd rearranged the furniture only a bit, creating the space needed for the new crib and changing table that had been delivered that day. She'd taken down the heavy drapes that hung at the windows, but had left the sheers in place. The drapes could easily be rehung, if Ace demanded it—although she sincerely hoped he wouldn't. Without the heavy fabric to block the light, the once dreary bedroom across the hall from Maggie's was now a cheerful, sun-filled space, perfect for a nursery.

Tired, but satisfied with the results of her afternoon's work, she crossed to the crib and reached down to pick up the baby. "And what do you think of your new room, precious?" she asked, turning and holding the infant against her chest so that the baby could see her new room. "Isn't it beautiful?"

Laura opened her mouth in a big, sleepy yawn.

Maggie laughed. "Well, it's a good thing I've got thick skin," she said, as she moved to sit down on the rocker. "Otherwise, your lack of enthusiasm would've hurt my feelings."

Shifting the infant to the crook of her arm, she pushed her toe against the floor and set the rocker into motion. Within seconds, Laura's eyelids, already heavy with sleep, fluttered down, her eyelashes curling tightly against her cheeks. Smiling softly, Maggie traced a finger beneath the furl of lashes, marveling at how much the baby had grown and changed in the few short weeks since her birth. She tried to imagine what Laura would look like as a young woman. Would she have her mother's fragile, waif-like beauty? Or had she inherited her bone structure from the Tanner side and would have high, sculpted cheekbones like Ace?

Ace.

At the thought of him, she dropped her head back with a groan. What was she going to do about him? He hadn't said more than a dozen words to her over the past week.

And when he did bother to speak to her, it was as he was going out the door, telling her not to wait dinner for him. His silence frustrated her almost as much as did his absences. How could she hope to foster a relationship between him and the baby, if he was never around?

Earlier in the week, she'd given serious thought to leaving, thinking that without her there to care for the baby, he would be forced to interact with Laura. But she'd discarded the idea, fearing that, if she did leave, Ace would do something desperate, like turn Laura over to the state's Child Welfare Department, rather than take care of her himself. Maggie shuddered at the thought of Laura being subjected to one of the nightmarish foster homes she'd lived in as a child.

You see yourself in this kid, don't you? Dixie had said. *You think by sticking with her, you can prevent happening to her what happened to you.*

Maggie felt a prickle of guilt, remembering her response. She hadn't denied Dixie's suspicions, thus avoiding a lie, but she hadn't confirmed them, either.

But the similarities were there for any fool to see.

Trisha Dean, Maggie's mother, may not have died after giving birth to Maggie, as Laura's mother had, but for all practical purposes she might as well have. Unfortunately, the parallels didn't stop there. Maggie's mother had led as loose and irresponsible a life as Laura's mother had; maybe even more so.

At fifteen, Tricia Dean was living on the streets, pregnant with Maggie and well on her way to becoming a drug addict. Within six months of Maggie's birth, she'd hooked up with a pimp, who kept her supplied with drugs in exchange for turning tricks for him. Within nine, her baby had been taken away from her and placed in a foster home.

But Tricia had never lost contact with her daughter, in spite of the number of times the social workers had moved

Maggie from one foster home to another. On a few occasions, she'd even convinced the social workers that she was clean and had persuaded them to return Maggie to her care. But those occasions were rare and never lasted long.

Raised by an ever-changing set of foster parents, by the age of twelve, Maggie was street-wise enough to recognize her mother's drug habit. The runny nose. The shaking hands. The unnatural thinness. What started out as resentment toward her mother, built over the years and slowly festered into hate. Maggie despised the dumps her mother lived in and the men who came and went at all hours of the night. But most of all, she despised her mother's weakness that made her choose a life of drugs and prostitution over one with her own daughter.

In the end, when Tricia was dying, her organs destroyed by the drugs she'd pumped into her system, she'd asked for Maggie. At first, Maggie had refused to see her mother. But she'd finally agreed to visit her, planning to say a quick "thanks for nothing," then split, severing a tie that had never existed in the first place.

But when Maggie had stepped inside the crowded hospital ward and seen her mother lying in the bed, the bitter words had dried up in her throat. There was nothing left of her mother but paper-thin skin stretched over protruding bones and hollowed-out eyes that stared at nothing. Her hair, what was left of it, stuck out in wild tufts that looked fried, as if she'd given herself a home perm and left the solution on too long. Wide, white restraining straps had bound her chest, hips and legs, leashing her to the bed.

Stunned by her mother's emaciated appearance and appalled by the bonds that held her prisoner, Maggie had sunk weakly down on the chair beside the bed. She had no idea how long she'd sat there, before her mother had turned her head on the pillow, and Maggie had looked into eyes the same tobacco-brown as her own. Recognition had flared for a moment in Tricia's eyes, followed by tears that dripped onto the pillow, chased there by a lifetime of wrong turns and regrets.

The sight of her mother's tears shouldn't have gotten to Maggie. Not after all the years of abuse and neglect. But for some stupid reason they had, and Maggie had ended up staying. She'd clung to her mother's hand while Tricia had screamed and fought the restraints, begging for the very drugs that were killing her. She'd wiped her mother's brow and wet her parched lips when Tricia's ranting would cease and she would slip back into a comatose state.

Hours had turned into days and days into weeks, with Maggie remaining by her mother's bedside, nursing her, while watching and praying for her death. As the chilling rattle of her mother's last breaths had echoed around her, Maggie had vowed then and there that she'd never make the mistakes her mother had made, that she'd never allow herself to become so dependent on anything or anyone that she'd sacrifice her life for them.

She'd slipped up once. A small slip that had almost cost her her self-confidence, her pride. Her sanity. But, thanks to Dixie, she'd managed to pull herself out of that dark hole and she'd started her life anew.

Blinking back tears as the memory faded, Maggie looked down at Laura. "But you'll never know that kind of pain," she whispered. "You're a Tanner."

Six

Avoiding someone who lived in the same house wasn't all that easy. Ace managed to pull it off by staying up nights sorting through the files in his father's office, then stumbling to bed in the wee hours of the morning and sleeping until noon each day. When he'd awaken, he'd head straight for town and spend his afternoons locked away in the offices of the family's lawyers and accountants, trying to get a handle on the Tanner assets and holdings. He'd already decided he was getting out of Tanner's Crossing and off the Bar-T as quickly as possible. But before he could, he had to make certain he could fulfill his duties as executor of his father's estate from his home in Kerrville.

From the hours he'd spent with the lawyers and accountants and those alone digging through his father's files, he'd determined that the bulk of the family's assets was comprised of real estate, most of which was raw land. Their holdings also included a number of office buildings, warehouses and a half-dozen or so apartment complexes in town, but those properties were all handled by a management company, so weren't a problem. The balance of the estate consisted of stocks, bonds and other "paper" investments that would require only occasional monitoring, which Ace knew from experience he could handle by phone or fax from anywhere in the world.

That left him with only the ranch to deal with. And until Ace hired a manager, one he could trust, it looked as if he was going to be stuck there awhile longer.

With Maggie.

Sighing, he pulled his truck to a stop in front of the ranch house and killed the engine. Leaning back against the seat, he rubbed a hand absently over his bandaged ribs as he looked over at the house. He knew she was inside, and knew, too, that he couldn't avoid her forever.

He owed her an apology. A big one. The things he'd said about Star…. He shook his head, a week later still shamed by the memory. All that talk about moral character. He hadn't meant a word of it. That had been his anger talking. His resentment. Most of which would've been better directed at his old man.

But without the old man there to take his frustrations out on, Ace had unloaded them on Maggie. He'd hurt her with the things he'd said. He'd known it immediately by the stricken look on her face, the angry way in which she'd lashed back. But he hadn't been able to stop himself.

To her credit, she'd fought back, and valiantly, striking him with blows where, he was sure, she thought she could hurt him the worst. He could still hear the accusation in her voice, the venom, when she'd told him that she hoped, if he ever got a woman pregnant, he'd turn tail and run. Little did she know that he never intended to get a woman pregnant, whether he was married to the woman or not. But she had managed to get in a hit when she'd accused him of not loving or caring for the baby just because the kid was a half sister and not a full sibling.

Half. Full. The degree of blood Ace shared with the kid wasn't what kept him from caring. He didn't *want* to care, didn't want the responsibility or heartbreak of taking on any more of his old man's screw-ups. He'd spent years running riot control over his old man's mistakes, smoothing out the upheaval caused by his father's selfish and careless acts, and he didn't intend to take on that role again. Ever.

But all that didn't matter, he told himself, and pushed open the truck door. Not now, at any rate. He had some crow to eat and putting it off wasn't going to make it any easier to swallow.

He'd expected to find Maggie in the kitchen, preparing the baby's bottles for the next day, as she did about this time every evening. When he didn't find her there, he headed straight for her room, hell-bent on getting his apology said and his conscience cleared before the sun set on another day. But he didn't find her in her room, either. Wondering where she'd gotten off to, he started to leave, but jerked to a stop, when he noticed that the playpen was missing from the foot of her bed.

Puzzled by its absence, he turned back to the hall. As he did, he saw that the door to the bedroom across the hall stood open. Usually closed, the open door was enough of an oddity to have him crossing to peer inside.

The room looked different, he thought, frowning. Lighter. Brighter. And the furniture wasn't where it was supposed to be. The bed, normally standing between the two windows, was shoved up against the far wall, and a crib now stood in its place. A table of sorts was bumped up against one end of the crib, a pile of diapers stacked high on its padded top. Wondering when Maggie had made the changes, he stepped inside.

And that's when he saw her. Sitting in the rocking chair,

her head resting against the chair's pressed back, her eyes closed, the baby asleep in her arms. With the chair angled in front of the window, the fading sunlight streamed across it, bathing both her and the baby in a hazy pool of golden light.

As he stared, a memory seeped slowly into his mind. One of his mother sitting in that same chair, rocking one or another of his brothers to sleep. Usually Rory, as he had always been difficult to settle down for the night. As she'd rock, she'd always sung a lullaby. Ace couldn't remember the words, but the tune played through his mind, as did the sound of her voice. Soft…melodious…soothing. As a youngster, he'd often sat out in the hall, his back to the wall, listening to the rhythmic creak of the rocker and the comforting sound of her voice, wishing like hell he was still small enough to crawl up in her lap to be rocked.

Even now, he could recall the contentment that would steal over him when she'd rocked him, feel the butterfly-soft comb of her fingers through his hair, the whisper of her breath against his cheek. She'd always smelled of roses, her breath of mint. Pleasant scents that, to this day, never failed to bring his mother to mind.

Slowly the memory receded and it was Maggie he stared at in the rocker. He wanted to be there, he realized, his throat closing around the urgency in that want. He wanted to sit in that old, oak rocker, with his hands gripped over the wooden armrests. He wanted to feel the wood's grain beneath his palms, a grain worn smooth by four generations of Tanner hands. He wanted to press his back against the narrow, oak slats carved by his great-great-grandfather and feel the sturdiness of the bowed wood giving beneath the pressure of his spine. He wanted to close his eyes and set the rocker into motion, letting its rhythmic movement lull his mind.

But he didn't want to be alone in the rocker, he realized

slowly. He wanted Maggie there, too. On his lap. He wanted the comforting weight of her head nestled in the curve of his shoulder, the warmth of her body curled against his. He wanted her fingers stroking over his face, her touch feather-light, slowly unraveling the tension from his mind and body. He wanted to feel the moist warmth of her breath on his face, the pillowed softness of her lips beneath his. He wanted to taste her seductive flavor, savor it...

Oh, God, he thought, balling his hands into fists against the need that twisted painfully inside him. He wanted *her*. Needed her more than he needed his next breath.

But Ace hadn't allowed himself to need anything or anyone in years. Wasn't even sure he could handle the level of emotion that kind of need generated, if he dared open himself up to it again. Knowing that, he remained just inside the door, scared spitless to take that first step toward her, yet wanting to so badly, it was a burning knot of pain in his chest.

As he stood, paralyzed by his fears, Maggie stirred and blinked open her eyes. A furrow creased her brow, as she slowly brought him into focus.

"Ace? Is something wrong?"

Her voice, husky with sleep and suffused with concern, seemed to wrap itself around his chest and squeeze. He shook his head, for a moment, unable to speak. "We need to talk."

Her frown deepened. "Now?"

"Yeah," he said, then added, "Outside," thinking, if he could just get out of this room and away from the memories it evoked, he could get a handle on his emotions.

Though she gave him a curious look, she didn't question his request. She simply rose and crossed to put the baby in the crib. After switching on the portable intercom hanging from the crib's top rail, she slipped a small monitor into her pocket and followed him out into the hall.

Ace led the way, acutely aware of the sound of her footsteps a few short steps behind. Once outdoors, he stopped to fill his lungs with the clean, fragrant air, praying it would release some of the tension that knotted his body, chase away the memories that still tangled in his mind.

When it did neither, he released the breath on a weary sigh. Giving his chin a jerk, indicating a field on his left, he said, "Let's walk."

Stuffing his hands in his pockets, he stepped off the porch and started off, leaving Maggie to follow.

By the time he had crossed the field and started up the low rise beyond it, the sun had sunk to a crescent of fire on the horizon that washed the landscape with the muted tones of twilight. At the top of the rise, he drew to a stop before a low iron fence, until that moment unaware that all along his destination had been his family's cemetery.

He heard the gentle fall of Maggie's footsteps behind him, the labored sound of her breathing as she struggled to catch up. When she stopped beside him, her arm brushed his sleeve and sent fractured shocks of awareness skittering beneath his skin. Gulping, he watched as she closed her hands over the finials that topped the iron posts and leaned to peer inside, the curl of her fingers around the delicately carved tops graceful. But he saw the red, work-roughened knuckles, remembered the hard life she'd led.

"Your family?" she asked.

Her voice, pitched low in reverence to the hallowed ground where they stood, whispered over him as gently as the evening breeze that stirred the leaves in the branches overhead.

"Yes." Fearing she would ask him why he'd brought her there and knowing that, if she did, he couldn't explain, he opened the gate and stepped inside.

Get FREE BOOKS and a FREE GIFT when you play the...

LAS VEGAS GAME

Just scratch off the gold box with a coin. Then check below to see the gifts you get!

YES!
I have scratched off the gold Box. Please send me my **2 FREE BOOKS** and **gift for which I qualify.** I understand that I am under no obligation to purchase any books as explained on the back of this card.

326 SDL DUYF

225 SDL DUYV

FIRST NAME	LAST NAME

ADDRESS

APT.#	CITY

STATE/PROV.   ZIP/POSTAL CODE

(S-D-03/03)

7	7	7	Worth TWO FREE BOOKS plus a BONUS Mystery Gift!
🍒	🍒	🍒	Worth TWO FREE BOOKS!
🔔	🔔	♣	TRY AGAIN!

Visit us online at www.eHarlequin.com

Offer limited to one per household and not valid to current Silhouette Desire® subscribers. All orders subject to approval.

Tombstones jutted from the ground at odd heights and uneven distances, their haphazard placement and mismatched appearance making them look like a hastily formed troop of untrained soldiers. Some stood straight and tall, while others tilted drunkenly, time and weather having taken their toll. A gray-green moss grew on the faces of the older stones, making the names and dates etched beneath indecipherable.

But Ace knew every name, date and epitaph by heart, having heard the family's history repeated to him over and over again through the years.

"General Nathaniel Johnson Tanner," he said, pointing, as Maggie moved to stand behind him. "'A brave and loyal soldier, mortally wounded leading his Confederate troop into battle.' He wove his way past several tombstones, careful not to step on any of the all but indiscernible graves, then pointed again. "Elizabeth Eddison Tanner and Infant Son Tanner. Left this earth July 20, 1872 and passed into heaven together, with my dearly beloved Lizzy carrying our babe to lay at the feet of our precious Lord and Master."

He walked on, pointing out the final resting places of his Tanner ancestors, his dispassionate tone that of a tour guide who had given this same spiel a thousand times or more.

Puzzled by his odd behavior, Maggie followed, wondering what he wanted to talk to her about and why he'd chosen a cemetery of all places to hold the conversation.

As they reached the newer section, he slowed, then stopped altogether before a mound of freshly turned earth. Assuming it was his father's grave that held his attention, Maggie maintained a respectful distance to give him whatever privacy he needed. But when he turned away to drop down on a stone bench positioned opposite the grave, she realized it was a stone to the right of the mound that had held his attention. Curiosity drew her close enough to read the words etched on the pink granite.

Emma Louise Tanner
Wife of ''Buck'' Tanner

She glanced over her shoulder at Ace. ''Your mother?'' His gaze fixed on the tombstone, he slowly nodded.

When he offered nothing more, with a shrug, she joined him on the bench, assuming that sooner or later he'd get around to telling her what he wanted to talk to her about.

While she waited, sitting quietly at his side, dusk descended around them, lengthening the shadows of the trees that bordered the fenced area. In the distance, a coyote howled, and the eerie sound sent a chill down Maggie's spine.

Anxious to return to the safety of the house, she thought a gentle reminder might speed things up a bit. ''You said we needed to talk.''

He roused, as if coming from a trance, to look at her. Frowning, he leaned over to pluck a wildflower from the ground at his feet. With his forearms braced on his thighs, he slowly rolled the stem between his fingers.

''About the other day,'' he began hesitantly.

Maggie knew, without asking, which day he meant. The afternoon at Star's and the beginning of what she'd come to think of as ''the silent war.'' ''Yes?'' she prodded helpfully.

''I—'' He stopped, frowned, then tried again. ''I'm sorry for the things I said about Star. I shouldn't have said what I did.''

''No,'' she agreed. ''You shouldn't have. You didn't know Star.''

''Whether I knew her or not, is irrelevant. I was mad and took it out on you. I'm sorry for that.''

Surprised by his apology, for a moment, Maggie couldn't think of a thing to say. ''Who were you mad at? Me?''

Scowling, Ace tossed the flower away. ''No. My father.''

He jerked his chin toward his mother's tombstone. "You'll notice there aren't any pretty words or touching epitaphs carved on my mother's stone. 'Wife of Buck Tanner,' he quoted, with a sneer. "As far as the old man was concerned, that was her one crowning achievement."

"But she was more than that to you. To your brothers."

Puffing his cheeks, he slumped back against the trunk of the tree. "Yeah," he said, releasing the breath on a shuddery sigh. "A helluva lot more."

In the field below them, a quail sang out its familiar call of, "bob-white, bob-white." For Ace, the sound brought back a wealth of memories that he suddenly found he wanted to share with Maggie.

"When we were kids," he said thoughtfully, "after dinner, Mother would let us play outside for awhile before shooing us all off to bed. She'd usually watch us from the front porch swing, while she rocked Rory to sleep. Sometimes, if she was lucky enough to get him down at a decent hour, she'd come out and play with us. Ring-around-the-rosy. Drop-the-handkerchief. Sissy, childhood games that my brothers and I wouldn't have been caught dead playing any other time. But we'd have played dolls with her, if she'd suggested it, just for the chance to be with her.

"She had a way about her that made even the simplest things fun. In the summer, when the garden was producing, she would ice down a watermelon. That evening we'd sit out on the porch steps and eat it, the meat of that melon so cold, it made our teeth ache. When we were done, she'd challenge us to a contest to see who could spit their seeds the farthest." He shook his head, chuckling, remembering. "Woodrow, Ry and I would just about kill ourselves, trying to outspit each other."

Maggie stared at Ace's profile, astounded by the wistful smile that curved his lips…and envious of his memories. "You must have loved your mother a great deal."

His smile slowly faded. "Yeah. I did."

"How old were you when she died?"

"Twelve. Cancer was what killed her. By the time the doctors found it, there was nothing they could do." He angled his head to look over at her. "Remember when you told me you thought the hospital staff treated your mother differently because she couldn't pay for her care?"

Maggie tensed, unsure why he was bringing the subject up again. "Yes. Why?"

"My mother got five-star treatment. A private room, her own nurse, gourmet meals cooked especially for her. The way I figure it, the wing the Tanners funded for the hospital earned her that kind of care." He looked away, turning his gaze to a darkening sky the setting sun had stained a red, burnished gold. "But there was one thing money couldn't buy her."

"What was that?"

"Time."

Maggie heard the regret in his voice, saw the longing in the face he tipped heavenward, and understood because she'd felt the same emotions when she allowed herself to think of her mother. "Was she in the hospital long?"

"A couple of weeks. Maybe three, if you stacked all the different stays into one. But she didn't die there," he added, glancing her way. "She wanted to die at home and in her own bed."

"That must have been difficult for your father."

"Buck?" Ace snorted. "It might've if he'd been around."

Maggie looked at him in puzzlement. "Your father's business required him to travel?"

"Rarely. He was usually shacked up with his current flavor of the month in an apartment he kept in Tanner's Crossing."

Maggie had heard Star mention the apartment, but she

was surprised that Ace knew about it, as well. That he did perhaps explained some of the bitterness he felt toward his father.

It also raised another question in her mind. "If your father wasn't home to take care of your mother, who did?"

"From six in the morning to ten at night, a private nurse the old man hired. The graveyard shift was mine."

"Yours?" she repeated in surprise. "But you were so young."

He lifted his shoulder in a shrug. "Age wasn't a requirement. In the beginning, I thought the chemo was the worst. After she'd have a treatment, she'd be so sick she could barely lift her head." He shook his head, as if at his own foolishness. "But I soon learned that the worst was the waiting."

"Waiting? For what?"

"Death."

A shiver shook Maggie, as she remembered waiting for her own mother's death, praying for it even, and how endless the nights had seemed, how lonely. When she looked at Ace again, he was staring off into space, as if at a distant memory.

When he spoke, his voice was so low she had to strain to hear his words.

"She was so scared. Sometimes I would hear her crying at night, and I would go to her room to check on her." He huffed out a derisive breath. "As if *I* could do anything. Hell, I was so wet-behind-the-ears, so useless, I didn't know what the hell to do or say. The only thing I could think of was to climb up into bed with her and snuggle close."

Emotion crowded Maggie's throat at the image of Ace comforting his mother. "It was what she needed," she told him. "Knowing someone cared. Having someone with her."

"Whether it was or not, it was all I knew to do."

Maggie's heart broke a little at the regret in his voice. "You miss her, don't you?"

His Adam's apple bobbing convulsively, he slowly nodded his head.

Tears filled her eyes. "Oh, Ace. I'm so sorry."

Ace tensed at the offer of sympathy. *I'm so sorry.* They were only words. Strung together, they were a common sentiment offered to someone who'd suffered the loss of a loved one. He figured he'd heard them voiced a hundred or more times over the last few days alone. But no one had offered them with the wealth of empathy and sincerity that Maggie had…and never with the same results. With those three simple words, she'd managed to reach deep down inside him and dredge up emotion from the vault he'd locked it away in years ago. It filled his throat, a knot of choking pain he couldn't seem to push a word past.

Ducking his head, he swallowed hard, trying to force the emotion back. As he did, he caught a glimpse of Maggie's hands fisted against her thighs, her knuckles now gleaming as white as pearls. In her tightly curled fingers, he recognized the same level of restraint he'd used to govern his emotions for years, the same heart-wrenching pain that had forced him to bury his emotions. Knowing that she'd suffered similarly, perhaps still did, touched him at a depth that nothing had tapped in years.

Reaching out, he covered her hand with his, laced his fingers through hers. Squeezed.

He heard the choking sound she made, felt the desperate clamp of her fingers around his. Angling his head, he saw the tears that flooded her eyes, the quiver of her lips. Helpless to do anything less, he hauled her to him and wrapped his arms around her.

With his hand cupped at the back of her neck, holding

her cheek to his, he felt each scalding tear that streaked down her face, absorbed each sob that racked her body.

But he didn't let her go. Couldn't. And when her tears stopped, he continued to hold her.

From the moment he'd dragged her into his arms, his only thought had been to give her what little comfort a jaded man like himself had to offer. But when her tears stopped, he found himself fisting his fingers in her long hair, drawing her head back, and sliding his mouth to cover hers. On her lips, he tasted the salt of her tears. Saddened by it, he swept his tongue over them to wipe them away. As he did, he felt the tremble that shook her, the unexpected surge of her breasts against his chest and, with a groan, he crushed his mouth over hers.

He kissed her deeply, greedily, taking each pleasure she offered up to him and claiming it for his own. He filled his hands with her hair, knotted his fingers in the dark, silky tresses, then let it slide through his fingers to skim his palms down her back.

With his hands gripped at her hips, he drew her hard up against him and slipped his tongue between her parted lips. He heard her whimper, felt the desperate dig of her fingers around his neck, and gave her more, took more of what she gave up to him.

Time became something indeterminable, the memories that had haunted him moments before nothing but hazy mists that slunk back into the dark recesses of his mind. His world shrank to the bench he sat on, inhabited only by the woman he held in his arms.

When he'd first reached for her, he'd sought only to ease her heart, absorb what he could of her pain. But he found that, somewhere along the way, she'd eased his and left him with a need so strong it thundered through his blood like a herd of wild buffalo, deafening him to all other sound and blinding him to all but her. Maggie.

His response to her stunned him. More, it scared the hell out of him. Holding her face between his hands, he forced their lips apart, until he met her gaze. Passion glazed her tobacco-brown eyes, stained her cheeks. He dropped his gaze to her mouth and to lips bruised from the pressure of his. Shamed by his rough treatment of her, he smoothed a thumb across them to soothe the swollen flesh…and had to wrestle with the temptation to kiss her again.

But Ace wasn't sure, if he did kiss her, he could leave it at that. Not when his body cried out for a much stronger release.

Drawing in a ragged breath, he lifted his gaze to hers. "We'd better head back. Morning's going to come early, and my brothers are due at daybreak to help me round up the cattle."

She gulped, nodded, slowly inching away from him.

As she stood, Ace stood, too, but reached out and caught her hand before she could move away.

"Maggie?"

She glanced back over her shoulder. "Yes?"

"I—" He stopped, searching for just the right words to convey how special he thought she was, how grateful he was to her for listening to him ramble on about a past he seldom allowed himself to even think about, much less share.

Unable to come up with anything that came even close to what he was feeling, he gave her hand a squeeze. "Thanks."

Eyes wide, Maggie lay in her bed, staring up at the ceiling where moonlight and shadows played a mystical game of hide-and-seek. Sleep was the farthest thing from her mind.

Who *is* this man? she asked herself for probably the zillionth time since crawling into her bed. She wasn't sure she knew any longer—if she ever had, at all. That night Ace had revealed to her a side of himself that she'd never dreamed existed. He'd given her a glimpse of a tenderness that she would never in a thousand years have suspected he kept hidden behind that cold and wary guard he kept in place.

And, God help her, she'd discovered in him a passion she prayed she would have the opportunity to experience again.

Pressing her fingers to her lips, she closed her eyes and tried to remember every detail. His masculine scent. The possessive tug of his hands in her hair. The urgent thud of his heart against hers. The burning rasp of his beard against her skin. The satin-like texture of his lips on hers. The seductive power of his touch, his kiss. The restraint she sensed beneath it all.

She recalled in vivid detail each and every breath they'd shared, every touch, every look, the thrill of his kiss, then played it through her mind over and over again.

And when, at last, she slept, it was Ace she dreamed of.

It was still dark outside, when Maggie started breakfast the next morning. Through the kitchen window she could see a hint of pink on the horizon, signaling dawn was quickly approaching, and along with it, the arrival of Ace's brothers.

Unsure if she was expected to feed them all, Maggie pulled a long tray of biscuits from the oven and set them on the island to cool, then turned back to the stove to shovel sizzling patties of sausage onto a platter. As she worked, she found her mind drifting back to the evening before and wondering how she could possibly face Ace again.

''Maggie?''

Startled, she dropped the spatula and whirled to find Ace

standing on the opposite side of the island. Bare-chested, he held a shirt in one hand and a roll of tape in the other.

She pressed a hand to her heart to still its pounding. "I didn't hear you come in."

"Sorry." He held up the roll of tape. "Since I'm going to be riding today, I thought I should wrap my ribs again. Would you mind doing it for me?"

Gulping, she wiped her hands down the skirt of her apron. "Just give me a minute to finish taking up the sausage."

She quickly turned back to the stove, praying Ace would think the flush on her cheeks was due to the heat from the stove.

Taking her time, she shoveled the remaining patties onto the platter. When she'd finished, she caught up a dish towel and wiped her hands, as she turned to face him again. "Now," she said, forcing a smile. "Let's see about those ribs."

He rounded the island and held out the roll of tape. "Something sure smells good."

To avoid looking directly at his chest, she peeled back a strip of tape from the roll. "I made sausage, biscuits and gravy. I wasn't sure if your brothers would have eaten yet, so I cooked enough for an army. You'll need to move your arms."

He lifted them out, holding them at shoulder level. "Probably wise. All the Tanners were blessed with healthy appetites."

As well as gorgeous bodies, she thought, trying not to stare as she pressed the end of the tape against the center of the most gorgeous chest in the world. Ducking under his arm, she began to wind the tape around his upper body.

When she'd circled him four times, she caught the tape between her teeth, starting a tear, then used her fingers to rip it from the roll. "There," she said, pressing the severed end into place. "All done."

He looked down at her and smiled. "Thanks. I couldn't have managed it alone."

Feeling the heat crawl up her neck, she mumbled a barely audible, "you're welcome," and started to turn away. He caught her arm, stopping her, and pulled her back around to face him.

"Maggie...about last night..."

She held her breath, praying he wasn't about to tell her he was sorry that he had kissed her, that it was a huge mistake he now regretted. "Yes?"

Catching her other arm, he drew her to him. "Last night was...special." He gave her arms a squeeze. "*You're* special."

She stared, not trusting her ears.

Ducking his head, he set his jaw, as if he had more to say, but was having a hard time saying it.

"I never talk about my family," he said hesitantly. "I guess because the memories are just too painful. Especially those of my mother." He looked up at her. "You're the first person I've ever told about her. The first one I felt would understand what it was like. I just want you to know how much that meant to me, how much I appreciated you listening."

At the time, Maggie had thought she'd realized how difficult it was for him. Sharing his emotions, baring his soul...that kind of openness would be foreign to a man like Ace. But she understood now what a monumental step that had been for him. She also knew that in talking about his mother and his past, he'd made a giant step toward healing his heart. A heart she prayed would open wide enough to accept Laura.

Hoping to encourage him to continue that healing process, she took a step closer and opened her hands over his chest. "I'm here, Ace. Any time you need to talk, I'm willing to listen."

He nodded. "I appreciate that." He seemed to hesitate a moment, then arched a brow and looked up at her over it. "I was kind of hoping you'd be interested in doing more than just listening."

She tensed, unsure of his meaning.

His smile tentative, he drew her to his chest. "Last night was special for another reason. We'd be good together. I think we both saw the proof of that."

"Y-yes. I suppose we did."

He frowned, as if only now considering the complications. "This could get dicey."

She wet her lips, her mouth suddenly dry. "If we were to allow it to, yes, I suppose it could."

He backed up a step, holding her far enough away that he could see her face. "I'm not looking to get married again."

She gulped, but nodded. "Me, either."

"And I travel all the time, rarely home for more than a week or so before I take off on another assignment."

"My studies keep me busy."

A smile spread slowly across his face. "Sounds to me like we have us a match made in heaven."

Before she could agree or disagree, he dipped his head over hers. Whatever doubts she may have harbored melted at the touch of his lips. Sliding her arms around his neck, she gave herself up to him.

Not only did their expectations align perfectly, she discovered, their bodies did, as well. Lips, chests, hips, thighs. Her curves molded against his body as naturally as if she'd been designed solely for that purpose.

His kiss, tender at first, as if testing, exploring, became more urgent, demanding. He ran his hands down her sides, then up again, bringing her T-shirt up with them. The pressure of his thumbs against the swell of her breasts was a delicious pleasure that made her nipples knot, aching for his touch.

Without warning, he tore his mouth from hers and looked toward the back door.

"Damn," he swore. "They're here."

Dazed, she blinked up at him. "Who's here?"

He reached for his shirt. "My brothers. Remember? They're coming to round up cattle today."

Before she could fully absorb what he was telling her, he dropped a kiss on her mouth, then grinned and shot her a wink. "We'll finish this later."

The back door opened and Maggie whirled, quickly snatching her shirt into place, sure that the word *guilty* was emblazoned across her forehead.

"'Bout time you boys showed up," Ace said, as he tucked his shirttail into his jeans, seemingly unfazed by the fact that his brothers had nearly caught him necking with the nanny in the kitchen. He lifted a hand to point at the first man through the door.

"The ugly one there," he said to Maggie, "is Dr. Ryland Tanner, better known around here as Ry."

Giving Ace a go-to-hell look, Ry peeled off his stained cowboy boot and tapped it against his thigh, as he nodded a terse greeting to Maggie. "Pleased to meet you."

"And this one," Ace said, catching the second one to enter in a headlock before he had a chance to fully clear the threshold, "is Woodrow." With every muscle in his neck standing out in relief as he strained to maintain the hold on his brother, Ace gasped out, "Remember? I told you about him."

Wide-eyed, Maggie stared. "Y-yes. The one who wrote the book on stubbornness."

With a low growl, Woodrow bent at the waist, dragging

Ace across his back, then came up with a bear-like roar, throwing his muscled arms wide.

"Stubborn, hell," he growled, flicking Ace off his back as if he were nothing more than a pesky fly. He hooked a thumb in Ace's direction. "*He's* the stubborn one. Me? I'm just cantankerous."

Rendered speechless by the display of strength she'd just witnessed, Maggie gulped. "I—it's nice to meet you, Woodrow."

He scooped a handful of biscuits from the tray on the island and popped one into his mouth. "Same here," he said around a mouthful, as he strode past her.

Winded, Ace smoothed his hair back into place, then gestured to the man who stood just inside the door, his back braced against the wall. "The shy, quiet one over there in the corner? That's Whit."

Realizing that the attention was directed his way, Whit whipped off his cowboy hat and snapped to attention, his cheeks reddening. "Pleased to meet you, ma'am."

Maggie smiled—warmly this time—enchanted by Whit's shy manners. "The pleasure's mine," she assured him.

Ace glanced over as Rory closed the back door behind him. "And this one," he said, with a careless wave, "you already know."

Relieved to see a familiar face—and a friendly one, at that—in the roomful of strangers, Maggie extended her hand. "Hey, Rory. It's good to see you again."

Rory let out a whoop and, ignoring the offered hand, scooped her up and off her feet.

"Not nearly as good as it is to see you," he cried, all but squeezing the breath out of her in a rib-cracking hug. Planting her on her feet again, he dropped a kiss full on her mouth, then lifted his head and sniffed the air. "Is that sausage I smell?"

Maggie pressed a hand against her forehead, her head

spinning dizzily. "Yes. And biscuits and gravy, too, if you're hungry."

Rory scrubbed his hands together, then pushed his arms out, as if to hold his brothers back. "Stand aside, boys, or be trampled. I'm fixin' to do me some serious grazin'."

He hadn't taken a full step toward the table, when Ace clamped a hand around his arm.

"Not now you're not," he growled. "We're headin' out."

Maggie looked at Ace, surprised by the anger in his voice.

Rory jerked free. "Who put the burr under your saddle?"

Snatching his cowboy hat from the rack by the door, Ace rammed it over his head. "Nobody. Now get your butt movin'. All of you. We've got work to do."

"But Ace," Maggie cried. "What about breakfast?"

Ace snatched open the door. "They came to work, not to eat," he muttered.

Woodrow, Ry and Whit dutifully followed Ace out the door. Rory headed for the island and the platters of food Maggie had left there.

"Who the hell does he think he is?" he grumbled, as he stuffed sausages into a stack of split biscuits. "Tellin' me what I can and can't do like I was still a snotty-nosed kid." He dumped the biscuits onto a napkin and brought the ends of the cloth up, tied them in a knot. "Well, we'll see whose butt is still movin' at the end of the day," he said smugly. Palming the napkin, he turned for the door, but skidded to a stop when he saw Maggie's stricken face.

"Now don't you go worrying that pretty little head of yours," he told her in that slow drawl of his. "I'm not plannin' on killin' him." He crossed to the door, opened it, then glanced back. "But I can't make any promises as to what that horse he's riding has in mind for him." Grinning, he shot her a wink and stepped outside, then shouted, "Hey, wait up! Y'all aren't leaving without me!" and slammed the door behind him.

With a shake of her head, Maggie crossed to the window, watching as Rory jogged toward the barn, where the others were already mounting their horses. As she did, she wondered if Rory's shout of "Y'all aren't leaving without me!" was one pulled straight from his childhood. She could imagine him, the youngest, always having to run to catch up with his older and bigger brothers.

And she could imagine, too, Ace ordering the others to wait while their little brother ran to catch up.

So what was with Ace's anger? she asked herself, still puzzled by it. Why had he been so rude to Rory, even refusing him the time to grab a bite to eat?

Unable to come up with a reasonable explanation, she focused her gaze on the brothers, as they prepared to ride out. Though they all shared a few physical traits in common, each was unique unto himself. Woodrow was definitely the largest, both in breadth and height. Remembering his claim of being cantankerous, she shuddered, doubting anyone would argue the point with him. He *was* cantankerous and scary to boot.

But Ry wasn't exactly Captain Sunshine, she thought, shifting her gaze to study him, though she suspected his surliness was due to impatience. She'd clued into his level of impatience immediately, noticing the tense way he held his mouth and the nervous way he tapped his hat against his thigh. And he was unhappy—or, at the very least, dissatisfied. How she knew that, she wasn't sure. Maybe it was the constant frown he wore. But what she didn't know was what made him unhappy.

A movement had her shifting her gaze away from Ry. Her heart softened a bit, as she saw Whit leading his horse off to the side, still a part of the group, yet slightly removed from the immediate circle of brothers. Was it his status as step-brother that placed him on the perimeter? she wondered. If so, were his brothers the ones who relegated him to the position of outsider or was it Whit, himself, who placed him there?

The dynamics were definitely interesting to consider, Maggie decided, as she watched the brothers turn their horses for the pasture.

She chuckled as she watched Rory swing himself up into the saddle and take out after the others, but grew thoughtful again, as she remembered Ace's rude treatment of him. Ace had greeted the others with a smile and a little good-natured roughhousing. But not so with Rory. The minute Rory had stepped through the back door, Ace had lit into him. And, as far as Maggie had been able to determine, Rory had done nothing to deserve his anger.

Had something happened between the two years before? she wondered. Something they'd never resolved and carried with them into adulthood?

Or could Ace possibly be jealous?

Intrigued by that possibility, she focused on Ace, in the lead. He rode with his hips slightly lifted and the balls of his feet planted firmly in the stirrups, distributing his weight evenly over the horse's back. Though a shirt covered his back now, she could well imagine him without it, her hands splayed over the pads of muscle, as they had been only short minutes before.

We'd be good together...

Shivering, she pressed her fingers against the glass, as if to reach out to him. Touch him.

Yes, they'd be good together, she thought. She didn't have a doubt about that.

But at what price?

She wouldn't allow a man to control her life again, no matter how tempting she found that man. And she would never jeopardize Laura's security and happiness for her own personal gain.

A match made in heaven? she asked herself, remembering Ace's words.

Or one destined for heartbreak?

Seven

Maggie had no idea what time to expect Ace and his brothers to return from rounding up the cattle. Rather than twiddle her thumbs, waiting—or wringing her hands and pacing, which was what she was afraid she might do—she filled her day doing the week's laundry and housework, mundane chores that unfortunately gave her way too much time to think of Ace and his last words to her.

We'll finish this later.

Since, prior to him making the comment, they'd been locked in a kiss, she had to believe that by *this* he'd meant the kiss. What haunted her was *how* he intended to finish it. The possibilities were endless, and each one she considered left her shivering in anticipation.

But as the clock slowly clicked away the minutes and hours, doubt crept in, her emotions running the gamut from breathless excitement to gut-wrenching fear.

Did she really want to get involved in a physical relationship with a man? she asked herself, as she rocked Laura to sleep for the night. After ending her disastrous marriage, she'd sworn off men, promising herself she'd never become dependent on another one for as long as she lived. But she was older now, she told herself. Wiser. She was aware of the pitfalls of dependency and knew that the amount of control she allowed a man to have over her life was up to her to establish…or withhold altogether.

But what about Laura? she worried next. How would Maggie's involvement with Ace affect the baby's future? Though she studied the possibilities from all conceivable angles, she couldn't think of a single way a relationship between the two could harm the baby.

With her concerns resolved for the moment, she continued to rock slowly back and forth, Laura having fallen asleep in her arms long ago. Without the lamp on, shadows draped the nursery. Worried that it would be dark soon, Maggie glanced out the window, but couldn't see anything six feet beyond the glass.

Hearing footsteps coming down the hall, she pressed a foot against the floor, stilling the rocker, and glanced toward the door, listening.

Oh, God, she thought, her panic returning. It had to be Ace.

Then he was there. In the doorway. His shoulders filling the space. Due to the lack of illumination, she couldn't see his face. Only his shape.

"Is she asleep?"

His voice, husky and deep, washed over her, a soothing balm to her burning nerves.

"Yes," she whispered. "Did y'all find all the cattle?"

"Most of 'em, I hope. We herded 'em all up to the north pasture where there's plenty of grass and water." He seemed to hesitate a moment, then asked. "Is she ready to put down?"

Maggie nodded, then rose and carried the baby to the crib to lay her down. Her sleep disturbed, Laura whimpered. Maggie leaned over the side of the crib, murmuring softly to her, patting her, until the infant had settled again.

She sensed Ace's presence beside her and glanced up. Their gazes met, her hesitation melting beneath the blue heat of his. Without a word, he took her hand and tugged her with him out into the hallway. Spinning her around, he crushed his mouth over hers and, with his body pressed against hers, backed her against the wall.

She tasted the need in him, the heat, saw it in his eyes, when, at last, he lifted his head to look down at her.

Smiling ruefully, he cupped a hand at her face and rubbed a thumb across the moisture he'd left on her lips. "I've been thinking about that all day. Kissing you. Nearly drove me crazy."

Mesmerized by the huskiness in his voice, the soft smile that curved his lips, she whispered, "Me, too."

He lifted both hands to her face, his expression turning earnest. "I want to make love with you, Maggie. I spent a hell of a lot of time thinking about that, too."

She closed her eyes, trembling, as he slid his hands down her arms and laced his fingers through hers.

"I thought about touching you," he whispered, brushing his lips across hers. "Kissing you, holding you." He dipped his nose into the curve of her neck and inhaled deeply. "Your scent haunted me," he murmured. "Roses." He opened his mouth and stroked his tongue over her flesh. "But you taste like sin."

Weakened by the seductive pull of his words, her body on fire from his touch, Maggie could barely stand. "Ace..."

Leaning into her, he slipped a knee between her legs. "Tell me that you want to make love with me, too."

The pressure of his thigh at the juncture of her legs sent

need rushing through her. Her mouth dry, her flesh afire, she could manage only a broken, ''Y-yes.''

Hearing the answer he wanted, he dropped his hands to her buttocks and brought her hips up hard against his. She felt the hardened length of his erection against her groin, nearly wept, as he found her mouth with his again. He kissed her passionately, thrusting his tongue deeply into her mouth.

He lifted her higher still, and she wrapped her arms around his neck and clung, as he carried her to his room. At the side of his bed, he stopped and loosened his hold on her, letting her body slide slowly down the length of his. When her feet touched the floor, she had to lock her knees to remain upright.

With a hand behind her neck, he drew back to rest his forehead against her. ''Damn,'' he moaned in frustration. ''I need a shower. I smell like the wrong end of a cow.''

She started to step away, but he tightened his grip on her, holding her in place.

''Take one with me.'' He dropped his mouth to hers and caught the hem of her T-shirt, drew it up. ''You scrub my back, and I'll scrub yours.''

She felt his teasing smile against her lips and couldn't help smiling, too. Fisting her hands in his shirt, she tugged it from the waist of his jeans and walked backwards as he urged her toward the adjoining bath.

He didn't bother with a light, but headed straight for the shower door. With his mouth still locked on hers, he reached around her to twist on the tap, then wrapped his arms around her and gave the kiss his full attention. Steam quickly filled the room, pearling on her already hot skin. He tore his mouth from hers and stepped back, ripping his shirt open.

Dragging in a ragged breath, Maggie stared at his bare chest. Unable to resist a moment longer, she splayed her hands over the muscled expanse, then smoothed them up, catching his shirt and dragging it over his shoulders. Tossing it aside, she carefully pulled off the tape she had bound him with earlier—with his chest bare now, she stepped into him, reaching for his belt as she pressed her lips over his heart.

Their movements became urgent, frantic, and soon they both were naked, their clothes scattered across the tiled floor. Holding up a finger, indicating for her to wait a second, Ace turned to pull open a drawer on the vanity. When he turned back, he held up a condom package for her to see.

"Protection," he said, and shot her a wink, then quickly ripped open the package. After fitting the condom over his erection, he caught her hand and guided her into the shower. He stepped in after her and closed the door behind him.

Steam filled the space, fogging the glass door and high window, while multiple showerheads sent hot, stinging streams of water to beat against their skin. With his gaze on hers, Ace took a bar of soap, rubbed it into a lather between his hands, then passed it to her. Maggie did the same, then moved in close, lifting her face to his, as she opened her hands over his chest.

Water streamed down their faces, as their lips met. Soap-slickened hands, combined with the needle-like sting of the water, added another level of sensuality to an already erotic act. Ace slid a hand between her legs, and she broke the kiss to suck in a breath, swamped by sensations she couldn't begin to name.

Murmuring softly to her, he cupped her buttocks and drew her to him, while stroking his finger along the seam of her feminine fold. Trembling, she dropped her head back and closed her eyes, giving herself up to the sensations. To him. She felt his mouth on her throat, the stroke of his tongue along her skin, both pleasure and torture. She gripped her hands at his shoulders to brace herself, as need swept through her in wave after drowning wave. He found her center, swirled his finger around the moist opening, then pushed inside. She arched, gasping, her body clamping down around him and pulsing wildly.

Desperate for him, she curled her fingers around his neck and brought his face down to hers. She drank deeply, thirstily, sweeping her tongue inside his mouth, seeking a satisfaction that she knew only he could give.

"I want you," she breathed against his lips. "I want to feel you inside me."

With a low growl, he lifted her, wrapping her legs around his waist, as he pressed her back against the tiled shower wall. With his mouth on hers, muffling her impatient whimpers, he thrust inside. He held himself there a moment, his body a rigid wall of restraint, giving her the time she needed to adjust to his size and length. He withdrew slowly, only to plunge again and again, setting a pace that Maggie was only too willing to follow. The sound of the water pounding against the tiles blended with the frantic rhythm of their bodies meeting, creating a symphony of sound that roared in their ears. The steam continued to billow around them, its heat pressing against their flesh, beading it with droplets of moisture that gleamed like diamonds in the mist.

Maggie felt the pressure building inside her, an impatient beast that paced and clawed, demanding release. Sure she would die if she didn't find relief soon, she locked her arms around Ace's neck and pushed her hips down against his. She felt the powerful lance of his manhood spear through her, the glorious explosion of her release, the pulsing throb of his…and melted weakly against his chest, her heart thundering against his.

Reaching up, she pushed her fingers through his hair and

turned her cheek to rub against his. "That was wonderful," she murmured.

He drew back to stare at her in disbelief. "Only wonderful?"

Laughing, she licked at the droplets of water that dripped from his chin. "Okay. Stupendous. Mind-blowing. The best sex I've ever had."

"Shoot," he scoffed. "That was nothin' but foreplay." Bracing her back against the tiles again, he dipped his head to capture a nipple between his teeth. He rolled his tongue around the stiffened orb, then released it to grin up at her. "I feel it's only fair to warn you. Tanners are known for their endurance."

She arched a brow. "Oh, really?" She slid her hand between their bodies, circling her fingers around him at the point where they joined. "Well, we'll see who outlasts who."

By Monday morning, Maggie was exhausted—if sated—and willing to call it a draw. After stepping from the shower Saturday night, she and Ace had dived into his bed and made love for what seemed like hours. Afterwards, they'd slept—not much longer than a nap, really—then made love again. And again. And again. And again. Sunday was a repeat performance, with breaks taken only when Laura was awake and needing Maggie's attention.

Shaking her head at the memory, Maggie scooped golden pancakes from the griddle and shoveled them onto waiting plates. She jumped, startled, when Ace slipped up behind her and wrapped his arms around her waist. Sighing, she sank back against him, as he nuzzled her neck.

"Good morning," he murmured sleepily.

Setting aside the spatula, she turned, looping her arms around his neck, as she smiled up at him. "Good morning to you, too."

He gave her a bone-melting kiss, then drew back and smacked his lips. "Mmm-mmm. You taste almost as good as those pancakes smell."

Laughing, she turned to switch off the burner beneath the griddle, then picked up the plates and led the way to the table. "Since I'm rather proud of my pancakes, I'll take that as a compliment."

He pulled out a chair and sat down opposite her, dragging a napkin over his lap. "Good. 'Cause I meant it as one." Picking up the syrup pitcher, he turned it up.

Maggie watched, her eyes rounding in amazement, as he drowned his pancakes in the thick sauce. "Would you like some pancakes with that syrup?"

Ace glanced up, then grinned and set the pitcher aside. "What can I say? I like sweets. I guess that's why I like you so much."

"Me? Sweet?" She choked a laugh. "That'll be the day."

He cut a triangle from his stack of pancakes and popped it into his mouth. "You are sweet," he said, then swallowed and added, "most of the time."

Jutting her chin, she poured syrup over her own pancakes. "Well, at least you're honest."

He leaned across the table and laid a hand over hers. "But you taste sweet all the time."

She narrowed an eye at him. "Are you trying to seduce me back into bed?"

"Is it working?"

Laughing, she waved her napkin in his face, shooing him back. "No. I've got too much to do to spend another day lazing around in bed with you."

Sulking, he sank back in his chair. "What do you have to do that's so all-fired important?"

"Well, for one, I have to take Laura to the doctor."

The color drained slowly from his face. "Is she sick?"

Maggie shook her head. "No. But it's time for her one-month check-up."

He blew out a breath and picked up his fork again, obviously relieved. "Tell 'em to send me the bill."

Maggie watched him sink his fork into another triangle of pancakes. "Ace?"

He glanced over at her. "Yeah?"

"Would you mind going with me?"

He dropped his fork to his plate and pushed out his hands. "Uh-uh. No way. You're not getting me anywhere near a doctor's office."

"But, Ace," she begged. "You're her guardian. Without you there to sign the necessary forms, they might refuse to see her."

Knowing she was probably right, Ace dropped his face into his hands, with a groan. "All right," he muttered and lifted his head to scowl at her. "But I'm not hanging around. Once I give whatever permission they need, I'm getting the hell out of there. Understand?"

Ace sat slumped in a chair in the clinic's waiting room, holding a fly fishing magazine in front of his face and trying his damnedest not to breathe any more than necessary. The antiseptic smell was already getting to him, making his stomach greasy.

Seemingly unaware of the sickening odor, Maggie sat beside him, cuddling the kid and whispering to her that there was nothing to be afraid of, that the doctor and nurses were her friends.

"Yeah, right," he muttered under his breath. "Try convincing the kid of that after they've poked and prodded her a few times."

The door beside the reception desk opened and the doctor stepped out, a manila file folder in his hand. "Laura Cantrell," he read from the folder's bright red tab.

Rising, Maggie called, "Over here," then stooped to gather the diaper bag. "Come on, Ace," she whispered. "It's our turn."

"Ace Tanner?"

At the sound of his name, Ace lowered the magazine to find the doctor looking at him curiously.

Frowning, Ace tossed the magazine onto the coffee table and stood. "Yeah. I'm Ace."

A smile slowly spreading across his face, the doctor started toward him. "Well, I'll be damned. Ace, I haven't seen you in a coon's age."

His frown deepening, Ace tried to place the guy. Slowly recognition dawned. "Tubby Clark?" he said in disbelief.

Wincing at the nickname, 'Tubby' glanced quickly around to make sure that no one had overheard. "Please," he begged. "It's taken me years to outlive that god-awful nickname. I prefer Ed or Doc."

"Doc, huh?" Grinning, Ace clasped Ed's hand, giving him a slow look up and down, as he shook. "Well, I reckon the name 'Tubby' doesn't fit anymore, anyway."

Chuckling, Ed smoothed a hand over a wash-board-flat stomach. "Medical school tends to do that to a man." Sobering, he slung an arm over Ace's shoulder and drew him toward the door. "I was sure sorry to hear about Buck, Ace. What a shock."

"Yeah. It was a shock, all right."

Ed opened the door, holding it for Ace and Maggie to pass through, then followed them. Indicating an examining room on his right, he led the way inside. "So what can I do for y'all?" he asked, obviously ready to get down to business.

Ace tipped his head toward Maggie and the baby. "The kid needs a check-up."

Ed blinked. "Damn, Ace. I didn't know you had any kids."

Scowling, Ace shook his head. "I don't. She's Buck's."

Ed stared a moment, then chuckled. "Looks like age didn't slow old Buck down any."

"No," Ace agreed, then gestured toward Maggie. "This is Maggie Dean, the kid's nanny. Whatever bill she runs up, you send to me."

Smiling at Maggie, Ed took the baby from her. "A nanny, huh?"

Maggie lifted a shoulder. "For the time being."

Figuring he'd done his duty, Ace headed for the door. "I'll wait out in the truck."

"Ace?"

His hand on the door, Ace glanced back to find Ed studying him critically. "Yeah?"

"Are you wearing a girdle or is that the outline of a bandage that I see beneath your shirt?"

Ace touched a hand to his ribs. "I ran into a little trouble with a horse."

Ed passed the baby back to Maggie. "Did the horse give you that cut on your face, too?"

Ace touched a self-conscious hand to his cheek. Though the wound no longer required a bandage, it hadn't healed completely. "Yeah. Must've landed on a rock or something when I fell. It's a lot better now, though."

Ed closed the distance between them. "Let me have a look at that." He poked at the skin surrounding the wound. "Who tended this?"

"Maggie. She's a nursing student."

Ed glanced over his shoulder at Maggie. "Really? We could use another good nurse around here. Are you interested in a job?"

"She *has* a job," Ace reminded him sourly.

Ed shrugged. "Doesn't hurt to ask." He motioned for Maggie to bring him the baby. "Here," he said to Ace, and passed the infant on to him. "You keep an eye on the baby, while I show Maggie around the office."

"Wait! I—"

The door closed behind the two, cutting Ace off. Muttering a curse, he strode to the examining table and laid the baby down. Bracing a hand on her stomach to keep her from falling off the table, he glared at the door.

Seconds later, it opened, and a nurse breezed in.

"Hi," she said cheerfully, as she placed a tray of supplies on the counter beside the examining table. "I'm Betty, Dr. Clark's nurse."

Ace eyed the tray warily. "Ace Tanner."

Giggling, she shifted his hand from the baby and began to unfasten the snaps on the baby's romper. "I know who you are, Mr. Tanner. Everybody does."

"Hey!" Ace cried, as she pulled the romper over the baby's head. "What do you think you're doin'?"

She gave him an absent pat. "Now, now. There's nothing for you to worry about. I'm just removing her clothes so that we can get an accurate weight measurement."

Lifting the baby, she laid the infant on the paper-lined tray above the scale and noted the weight. "Nine pounds," she told Ace, as she returned the baby to the examining table. "I'll take a quick blood sample, then we'll have her all ready for the doctor."

Ace paled. "Blood sample? Why do you need a blood sample?" Betty plucked a lancet from the tray, then caught the baby's heel and swiped it with an alcohol-soaked gauze pad. "The doctor requires one for all new babies."

Wedging himself between the nurse and the table, Ace bodily shoved her out of the way. "You're not sticking this kid with any needles," he told her, then lifted his head and yelled, "Maggie!" at the top of his lungs.

She made a tsking sound. "Now, Mr. Tanner," she

scolded, "there's no need to cause a scene. It's just a little prick."

"Little prick my ass," Ace muttered, then yelled again, "Maggie! Get in here!"

In spite of her diminutive size, Ace discovered that Betty was surprisingly strong...and quick. In the blink of an eye, she'd shouldered Ace aside, caught the baby's ankle and pricked the heel with the lancet. While Ace watched, too paralyzed to do anything more than stare, she squeezed, catching on a specimen slide the droplets of blood that bubbled from the small cut.

Laura let out an indignant wail.

With a growl, Ace snatched the baby up. Cupping a wide hand behind the infant's head, he turned his back on the nurse and hugged the baby to his chest. "It's okay, precious," he soothed. "Ace isn't going to let that mean old nurse hurt you again."

Fisting her fingers in the hair on his chest, Laura buried her face in the curve of his neck and sobbed pitifully. Ace gulped, mortally afraid that he might cry, too.

The door flew open and Maggie rushed in. "What's wrong?" she cried in alarm.

Ace spun to look at her accusingly, the baby held protectively against his chest. He jerked his chin toward Betty who cowered in the corner. "That crazy woman stabbed the kid and made her bleed."

Maggie couldn't decide which shocked her more: seeing Ace standing with the baby clasped against his chest, or the fact that he was standing at all, and not lying on the floor in a dead faint. Drawing in a careful breath, she moved to ease the baby from his arms.

"The nurse was only doing her job," she said quietly, in an effort to calm him.

"Since when is bloodletting a job?"

Ed stuck his head in the door. "Are y'all ready for me yet?"

Setting his jaw, Ace marched to the door. "Do you know what that damn-fool nurse of yours just did?"

Oblivious to what had transpired during his absence, Ed looked from his nurse to Maggie, then back at Ace. "No. What?"

"She stabbed the kid's foot with a needle the size of a first-grader's pencil."

Biting down hard on his lip to keep from laughing, Ed took Ace by the arm. "A first-grader's pencil, huh?" he said, as he pulled Ace out into the hall.

"You think this is funny?" Maggie heard Ace cry before the door closed behind the two men.

Still shaken, Betty looked over at Maggie. "Does he always act this crazy?" she whispered.

"Unfortunately, no."

At Betty's confused look, Maggie shifted the baby to her shoulder to give the nurse a reassuring pat. "Believe me. For Ace, this kind of crazy is a *good* thing."

Later that evening, Maggie set up the infant tub on the vanity in the bathroom off the nursery and proceeded to give Laura her nightly bath.

"So what do you think of your new tub?" she asked the baby, as she drizzled water over the infant's tummy. "Beats the heck out of that old kitchen sink at my house, huh?"

Squealing, Laura kicked her feet, splashing water on Maggie's face.

Laughing, Maggie tickled the infant under her chin. "You little scamp," she scolded playfully. "You're the one who's supposed to be getting a bath, not me."

She reached for a towel to blot the water from her face, but froze when she caught a glimpse of Ace's reflection in the bathroom mirror. He was standing in the doorway behind her, watching.

At some point during the evening, he'd shed his shirt, boots and socks, which left him wearing only his jeans. He'd left the top button on the jeans undone and, standing as he was with his hands braced high on the jamb and one knee cocked, his jeans rode low on his hips, accentuating the V of dark hair that arrowed down his abdomen and disappeared beneath the waist of his jeans. A patch of denim to the left of the jeans' fly was worn a lighter shade of blue.

"Is she okay?"

Realizing that she was staring—and *what* she was staring at—Maggie gulped, then gave him a reassuring smile. "She's fine."

He dropped his arms and moved to look down at the baby.

"No sign of any infection?"

Chuckling, she caught Laura's foot and lifted it up for him to see for himself. "You can't even tell where Betty pricked her with the needle."

He placed a hand over his stomach, blanching at the word "needle."

"Please," he begged.

Laughing, she drew Laura from the tub and quickly wrapped her in a towel. "You should be proud of yourself," she told him, as she led the way back into the nursery.

"Proud? Of what?"

She laid Laura down on the changing table and began to dry her off. "You didn't faint today at the doctor's office."

Scowling, he passed her a diaper. "I wish to hell Rory had never told you that story."

"I'm glad he did," she said, as she slipped the diaper beneath Laura's bottom. "I thought it was kind of sweet."

"Sweet?" He snorted a breath. "More like humiliating."

"Look at it this way," she told him, as she pressed the plastic tabs into place, securing the diaper. "A few more trips with Laura to the doctor, and you'll probably lose your fear of needles altogether."

"Yeah, right."

"It's true," Maggie said, as she guided the infant's arms through the sleeves of a gown. "It's a proven fact that the more often a person experiences something, the less frightening it becomes." She picked up the baby and pressed her against Ace's chest. "Here. Hold her a minute while I rinse out her tub."

Ace looked down at the baby, wondering how he'd ended up with the kid. Frowning, he trailed Maggie into the bathroom. "Do you think she's running a fever? She feels awfully warm to me."

Maggie tipped the tub over, dumping the soapy water into the sink. "If she feels warm, it's probably from the bath." She flipped the tub upside down over the sink to dry and turned to Ace, wiping her hands across the seat of her pants. "Would you like to give her a bottle, before I put her to bed?"

Ace opened his mouth to say no, but closed it and nodded his head instead. "Why not? You could probably use the break."

Hiding a smile, Maggie headed for the door. "It'll take me a minute to warm it up," she called over her shoulder. "Make yourself comfortable."

Ace glanced around. Not seeing any place in the bathroom to sit other than the commode seat, he walked back into the nursery and sat down on the rocker. "What do you think?" he asked the baby. "Is this comfortable enough for you?"

Laura squealed, flapping her arms wildly. Ace panicked, fearing he'd done something wrong.

"Now don't turn on the waterworks," he said nervously. "If you don't like this chair, I'll find us someplace else to sit."

She stilled and stared up at him, as if hanging on his every word. He gave his chin a jerk. "Well, you're going to like it even better once we get snuggled in." Careful not to startle her, he shifted her to a more comfortable position, then eased back, settling his spine against the rocker's bowed slats. "Now," he said, releasing the breath he'd been holding. "That's even better, isn't it?"

Yawning, she brought a fist to her eye and rubbed.

"Are you sleepy?" he asked. "Want me to tell Maggie to speed that bottle up?"

"No need," Maggie told him, as she entered the room. "I've got it right here." Smiling, she handed it to Ace, then sank down at his feet, watching as he offered it to Laura.

"She won't last long," she whispered, noticing that Laura's eyelids were already growing heavy. "She's had a pretty exciting day."

Ace nodded, fascinated by the tiny fingers that curled around his over the bottle. He lifted one of his fingers and carried three of hers up with it. Shaking his head, he lowered it back to the bottle. "She's so damn tiny."

Maggie laughed softly. "Most babies are."

"I suppose, though she seems exceptionally small."

"Dainty," Maggie corrected.

"More like fragile," he said, frowning down at Laura.

Chuckling, Maggie reached to blot a drop of drool from the corner of the infant's mouth. "Don't let her size fool you. She's tougher than she looks."

Ace snorted. "You're going to have a hard time convincing me of that." He lifted his finger again, drawing

Laura's entire hand up with it. "Just look at the size of that, will you? I've seen dolls with bigger hands."

"She'll grow," Maggie assured him. "She's already almost doubled her weight."

"Doubled!" he repeated, then winced, when Laura released the nipple and let out a cry. "Sorry," he murmured, as he guided the bottle back to her mouth. When she'd settled and began sucking again, he looked over at Maggie. "Doubled?" he said again, but more quietly this time.

Maggie nodded. "She weighed a little over five pounds at birth, and today she weighed in at nine pounds."

Ace blew out a breath. "Man. I had no idea she weighed less than five pounds at birth. That's small."

"Dainty," she reminded him.

"Fragile," he insisted.

With a shrug, she conceded the point. "All right, have it your way. But, like I said, she's tougher than you think."

"Look," he whispered. "She's already asleep."

Maggie rose to her knees and eased the bottle from the baby's mouth. "You can put her to bed now."

He looked up at her. "Me?"

She pushed to her feet and gave him a droll look. "It isn't as if you haven't done it before," she reminded him.

He looked down at the baby. "I did, didn't I?"

Careful not to wake her, he rose and crossed to the crib. He patted her back a moment, listening for her burp, then leaned over to lay her down. As he slipped his hand from beneath her, a hint of a smile curved the sides of the baby's mouth.

"Look," Ace whispered. "She's smiling."

Maggie draped an arm over his shoulders, as she peered down at the baby with him. "She's talking to the angels," she said softly.

He glanced over at her, his brow creased in puzzlement. "What?"

She shrugged. ''It's something I heard somewhere. Supposedly, when a baby smiles while she's sleeping, it means she's talking to the angels.''

Bracing his arms along the rail, Ace stared down at the baby. ''Whether it's true or not, it's kind of a neat thought.'' He reached down to tuck the blanket more securely around her. ''Do you think she's warm enough?''

Chuckling, Maggie hugged him against her side. ''Will you quit worrying? She's going to be just fine.''

Eight

At some point over the last two weeks, Maggie's plan to keep Laura's integration into the Tanner household as unobtrusive and subtle as possible had fallen by the wayside. Now a person couldn't take a step without dodging some type of infant gear. Another visit to town had produced a new playpen that had taken up permanent residence in the den. Baskets filled with an assortment of stuffed toys, teething rings and rattles were scattered all over the house, making the search for an item with which to entertain the baby as simple as reaching out a hand. On the floor of what Maggie considered Ace's office, a quilt was spread, its colorful squares embroidered with caricatures of different farm animals.

The biggest surprise of all, though, was that it was Ace who was responsible for the majority of the additions. He rarely made a trip to town that he didn't return with something new for Laura. An adorable chenille teddy bear for her to sleep with. A rubber rattle shaped like a dog's bone for her to chew on. A storybook constructed from fabric squares and illustrated with colorful felt appliques. With each new addition, Maggie silently prayed that it was a sign that Ace was moving closer to accepting the baby.

She was sending up a similar prayer one evening, when the doorbell rang. Her hands in dishwater, she lifted her head, listening to see if Ace would answer it. Not hearing a sound from his office, she quickly grabbed a dish towel and dried her hands as she hurried for the door.

Opening it, she found a delivery man on the porch. She looked at him in surprise. "It's rather late for a delivery, isn't it?"

"Not when we're transporting perishable goods." He glanced down at the clipboard he held. "The invoice is addressed to an Ace Tanner and requires a signature."

Since Ace hadn't responded to the doorbell, Maggie assumed he was busy and didn't want to be disturbed. "He can't come to the door right now. Is it okay if I sign for the package?"

The man handed over the clipboard. "Makes me no never mind. Personally, I'll be glad to get rid of the dang thing."

She quickly signed her name, then passed it back, frowning. "Why? Is it heavy?"

He snorted a breath. "Heavy and *loud*. The mutt hasn't shut up since I loaded the carrier into my truck."

Maggie's eyes bugged. "Mutt! Ace never said anything about buying a dog. Are you sure you have the right address?"

The man thumped the back of his hand against the clipboard. "Says it right here in plain black and white. Ace Tanner, Bar T Ranch, Tanner Crossing, Texas."

"That's the correct address, all right." Catching her

lower lip between her teeth, she strained to look around him. "Is the dog very big?" she asked uneasily.

He snorted a breath, as he turned and jogged down the porch steps. "Depends on what you call big."

Maggie watched as he slid open the truck's side door and disappeared inside. When he reappeared, he was stooped beneath the weight of a pet carrier large enough to contain a full-grown mountain lion. Maggie crossed to the edge of the porch. "Leave it there," she said, fluttering a hand at a spot on the sidewalk a good ten feet from the edge of the porch.

He groaned, straining, as he set the carrier down. "With pleasure." Dusting off his hands, he turned for his truck. "And good riddance."

Her gaze on the carrier, Maggie slowly descended the steps. She sank to her knees and stooped to peer inside. A yelp from the dog, had her jerking back. Placing a hand over her heart to still its beating, she stooped again to peer inside. A long, pink tongue snaked out and, before she could dodge it, licked her full on the mouth.

Curling her nose in disgust, she drew back, dragging the back of her hand across her mouth. "If I'd wanted a kiss," she complained to the dog, "I'd've asked for one."

His response was a pitiful whimper.

Her heart melting at the heartbreaking sound, she reached for the carrier's latch. "I bet you're tired of being inside of that old cage, aren't you, buddy? I'll let you out, but you've got to promise me you won't—"

Before she could finish the warning, the door flew open and a mountain of fur shot out, striking her against the chest and knocking her flat on her back. With her eyes squeezed shut, Maggie pushed at the dog, who seemed determined to thank her for rescuing him by licking her to death.

"Get off of me!" she cried, shoving at the dog. "You weigh a ton!"

"Not quite a ton, but close."

Hearing Ace's voice, Maggie flipped open her eyes, just as he collared the dog and pulled it back.

Afraid that he intended to punish the dog, she pushed up to her elbows. "He didn't mean any harm," she said, in the dog's defense. "He was just being friendly."

"'He' is a 'her,' and I've never laid a hand on her." He hunkered down and gave the dog's head a brisk rub. "Have I, girl?"

Maggie watched, her eyes widening as she recognized the dog. "That's the dog from the pictures you took for your book on Wyoming wildlife!" she cried.

Laughing, Ace tipped his head back, trying to dodge the dog's tongue, as it frantically licked at him. "This is her, all right...though there's a whole lot more of her. I left her with a buddy of mine in Kerrvile when I got the call that the old man had died. Since it looks as if I'll be here awhile longer, I asked him to ship her to me. Down, Daisy," he ordered sternly. Trembling with excitement, the dog immediately sat back on her haunches, her brown eyes fixed adoringly on Ace.

With a woeful shake of his head, Ace stood and offered Maggie a hand up. "Sorry about the exuberant greeting. She usually has better manners than that."

Maggie stared up at him, as he pulled her to her feet. "You had the dog all along," she said in disbelief. "Why didn't you tell me?"

He lifted a shoulder. "You didn't ask."

Before he had a chance to prepare himself, Maggie threw herself at him. With her legs wrapped around his waist and her arms around his neck, she peppered his face with kisses.

"I just *knew* you were hiding a heart somewhere in that gorgeous chest of yours."

Ace drew back to look at her askance. *"Gorgeous?"*

Maggie ducked her head, blushing to the roots of her hair. "Well...it is to me."

Dropping his head back, Ace hooted a laugh. "Gorgeous," he said again, then laughed even harder. "I don't think anyone's ever referred to my chest as *gorgeous* before."

Scowling, she squirmed, trying to get down. "I don't see what's so funny."

"I do. Gorgeous is a word used to describe a woman's looks. You know, like, 'Maggie Dean is one gorgeous chick.'"

She stopped squirming to look at him in wonder. "You think I'm gorgeous?"

"No. It was just an example."

"Why, you—"

Laughing, he dodged the fist she swung at his head. "I was only kidding!"

She eyed him skeptically. "Double-dog swear?"

"Triple-dog swear." He slowly eased her to her feet, but kept his arms locked around her. "Forgive me?"

"I don't know," she grumbled, unsure if she was ready to forgive him yet.

"Where's the kid?"

"Asleep."

He swept her up into his arms. "Good. That means I've got plenty of time to convince you."

"Ace!" she cried, clinging to his neck. "What about the dog?"

He stopped at the door, whistled and the dog came bounding up the steps.

"Stay, Daisy," he ordered, and the dog immediately flopped down on the porch and dropped her head between her front paws.

Maggie stared at the dog over Ace's shoulder, as he carried her inside. "Amazing," she murmured.

"I've always thought I was."

She bopped him on the back of the head. "Not you, goofus. The dog."

Reaching his room, Ace dumped her onto his bed, then dove in after her, wrapping his arms around her and pulling her over him, as he rolled to his back. "While I'm convincing you to forgive me, I guess I'll just have to convince you that I'm amazing, as well."

Enchanted by this playful side of Ace she had never seen before, Maggie planted an elbow on his chest. "And how do you intend to do that?"

"I could start by dazzling you with my magic skills."

She eyed him dubiously. "What magic skills?"

"I can make things disappear right before your eyes."

"What kind of things?"

He caught the hem of her T-shirt. "My specialty is clothing. Shut your eyes," he instructed.

She narrowed them at him instead. "You said '*before* my eyes.'"

"Semantics. Now close 'em."

Maggie obediently closed her eyes. In a flash, Ace ripped her T-shirt up and over head.

"You can look now."

When she did, he opened his hands before her face and turned them this way and that.

"See?" he said smugly. "No shirt."

She feigned a bored look. "Impressive, but not particularly amazing."

"Well, what about this?"

In the blink of an eye, Maggie was beneath him and the remainder of her clothes—as well as his—were on the floor.

"Now," he said, as he settled between her legs, winded by the effort. "What do you have to say about that?"

Smiling, Maggie slid her hands over his buttocks and urged him to her. "I'd say you're a master magician."

He fumbled a hand in the drawer of the bedside table, found a condom and put it on.

She gasped, tensing, as he pressed his erection against her center, then hummed her pleasure, melting around him as he slipped inside.

"Now *that*," she said, "is truly amazing."

She felt his smile against her neck, the rasp of his tongue as he stroked it down.

"Baby, you ain't seen nothin' yet," he said, just before he caught her nipple between his teeth.

She arched high as he suckled, then strained higher still, as he closed his hand around her opposite breast, mimicking with his fingers the seductive pull of his mouth on the other. Sensation churned inside her, gathering in speed and intensity until they melded into a single bolt of lightning that ripped through her body, piercing her low in her belly and creating an explosion that sent her flying over the edge.

She clung to Ace, her hands trembling, her heart thundering in her ears. "Ace!" she cried.

He chuckled and began to move inside her. "Like I said. Baby, you ain't seen nothin' yet."

A baby's cry tugged Maggie away from her dreams. Responding instinctively to the sound, she pushed back the sheet and started to rise.

A hand on her shoulder stopped her and pulled her back down.

"I'll check on her," she heard Ace say.

Murmuring gratefully, she snuggled her cheek into the pillow and dragged the sheet back to her chin.

When she awoke the second time, the first faint rays of sunshine were seeping through the drapes. Unwinding the tail of the shirt that was twisted around her knees, she smiled, remembering growing cold in the night and Ace getting it for her. Touched by his thoughtfulness, she stretched, rolled...then froze. Ace lay next to her, his face relaxed in sleep, his body curled protectively around the baby, who slept between them, a pacifier dangling from the corner of her mouth.

She gulped, swallowed, emotion crowding her throat. *Oh, Ace,* she thought, touched by the sight of them sleeping together. *Please, please, please let this be a sign that you've decided to keep her.*

Reaching out, she shaped a hand over his cheek and smiled as he blinked open his eyes to look at her. "This is a bad habit to start, you know," she warned.

He glanced down at the baby, then covered Maggie's hand with his and closed his eyes. "She was lonely."

Maggie chuckled and snuggled closer. "She said that?"

He shook his head. "No, but I could tell."

Her heart melting, Maggie leaned to press her lips to his. "You big softie."

"Uh-uh. Lazy. It was easier to stick her here, than have to stay up and entertain her."

Laura stirred between them, and the pacifier slipped from the corner of her mouth. Scrunching up her face, she let out an indignant wail.

Ace pulled his pillow over his head. "Your turn," he mumbled from beneath it.

With a rueful shake of her head, Maggie rolled to her knees and gathered the baby into her arms. "It's okay, precious," she soothed, as she scooted from the bed. "Maggie'll have you a bottle warmed before you can say scat."

"Scat."

Maggie glanced back to frown at the bed. "Very funny, Ace. Keep it up and you'll be the one doing the warming."

A snore came from beneath the pillows.

Chuckling, she headed for the door again. ''You big faker.''

The next two weeks passed in a blur of activity for Maggie. She spent one entire weekend doing nothing but cleaning the bunkhouse in preparation for the arrival of the three ranch hands Whit had managed to locate. The second she spent cooking and cleaning up after the hands, Ace and his brothers, who he had called home to help work the cattle. The men had worked from dawn until dusk on both Saturday and Sunday, first moving the cattle to the corral, then checking them over, doctoring those that needed it and castrating a dozen or more bull calves that—from the fuss they kicked up—weren't too crazy about the idea of being neutered.

On the weekdays in between, she cared for Laura and, in her spare time, helped Ace clean out his father's office and bedroom. She discovered that, for a man with such extensive holdings, Buck Tanner kept pitifully few records. Ace said it was because Buck didn't trust anyone, including his sons. Whatever his reasons, Buck had left few paper trails for Ace to use as a guide.

From the ranch hands Whit had located, Ace had learned that Buck had fired them all more than three months before his death. As to his reasons for doing so, the ranch hands didn't have much to offer, saying only that Buck had changed, turning meaner than was considered normal for even him, and had taken to sticking fairly close to the ranch.

In spite of all the extra work, Maggie had never been happier. She had Laura and she had Ace, the two people she'd grown to care about more than she'd ever expected to care about anyone again. The two people she was slowly beginning to think of as her family.

She knew it was wrong, dangerous even, to think of them in those terms. But she couldn't help it. She was sharing a home with them, cooking and caring for them, providing for their needs the same as a wife and mother would those of her family. And she slept with Ace. Shared his bed. Made love with him.

Granted, she'd told Ace from the first that she wasn't interested in getting involved in a relationship again and, later, that she wasn't interested in remarrying. For the most part, the last was still true.

Or was it?

She stole a glance at Ace, who, at the moment, sat slumped on the den sofa beside her, watching a movie, the fingers of his right hand laced with hers, his stockinged feet propped alongside hers on the coffee table. Did she want to marry Ace? she asked herself honestly. She mentally gave herself a shake and turned her gaze back to the TV. No. She couldn't think like that…not when he'd said nothing to make her believe he'd changed his feelings on the subject.

Yet, the question continued to niggle at her.

"Ace?"

His attention on the movie they were watching, he drew her hand to his lips. "Yeah?" he said absently.

"What will you do when you…well, when you finish up here?"

He moved his shoulder against hers in a shrug. "Go home, I guess." He turned to look at her. "Why?"

She looked quickly away and shook her head. "I don't know. I was just wondering."

He stared at her a moment, then turned to watch the movie again.

Maggie assumed he'd forgotten all about the question, until later that night, when they were in bed, and he asked, "Are there any nursing schools near Kerrville?"

She tensed, not daring even to breathe, knowing that Kerrville was his home. "I don't know," she said, praying her response came across with the indifference she tried to inject into her voice. "Why?"

He rolled onto his side and draped an arm over her waist, tugging her close. Pressing his lips to her temple, he murmured, "'Cause I was thinking you might want to consider transferring there and moving in with me."

She let the breath out slowly, her heart thundering within her chest. "I think there's a school in San Antonio, but I'm not sure."

He nuzzled his nose against her hair, then settled his head on the pillow next to hers and slid his foot between hers. "Wouldn't hurt to check it out."

"No. I suppose it wouldn't."

He yawned, then brushed his lips across hers. "'Night, Maggie."

She gulped, then whispered, "Good night, Ace." She listened as his breathing grew rhythmic, wondering how he could possibly sleep after making such a life-changing suggestion.

Sleep, for her, didn't come for hours.

At the sound of the phone, Maggie glanced up from the box of papers she was sorting. "Want me to answer it?" she asked Ace.

Sighing, he closed the drawer he was digging through. "That's okay. I'll get it."

Stretching across the desk, he plucked the receiver from the base. "Ace Tanner."

He listened a moment, a frown furrowing his brow. "Are you sure?" he said into the receiver, then listened again. He glanced toward Maggie, his frown deepening. "I don't know," he said slowly. "I'll have to do some checking and get back to you."

Replacing the receiver, he sank back in the chair, templing his fingers thoughtfully against his mouth.

"What?" Maggie asked, her curiosity aroused.

Dropping his hands, he shook his head. "That was the detective I hired to trace Star's family. He said the name 'Cantrell' was assumed."

"What!" Maggie cried. "But Star said—"

He patted a hand at the air. "I know. She told you her name was Cantrell. But the detective thinks she changed her name. He said he's traced her back to Las Vegas, but the trail dries up there, which makes him think she assumed the name there. He's following up on that theory now."

Maggie stared, unable to believe that Star had lied to her about her identity.

"What about Dixie?" Ace asked. "Wouldn't she have to have some kind of proof of Star's identity for her employment records? A social security number or something?"

Maggie pressed a hand against her forehead, trying to absorb the fact that Star had lied to her. "Yes. I suppose. Do you want me to call and ask her?"

Ace shook his head. "No," he said, rising. "It might be best if I talked to her in person."

Carrying the baby, Maggie led the way into the bar. Though it was still early in the afternoon, several customers already sat at the bar, nursing drinks, their eyes glued to the television anchored high on the wall in the corner. Donnie Gay, the announcer for the televised rodeo, was giving a play-by-play of a bull rider's eight-second ride.

Maggie spotted Dixie weaving her way through the tables toward them and offered a smile.

"Hey, Dixie," she said, as Dixie reached her.

Scowling, Dixie took the baby from Maggie's arms. "Hey, yourself." She glanced at Ace, gave him a quick once-over, then turned to Maggie without ever acknowledging his presence. "What are y'all doing here? Slumming?"

Surprised by Dixie's rudeness to Ace, Maggie glanced over at him. "Hardly." She turned to look at Dixie again. "Ace wants to talk to you. About Star," she added.

Dixie snorted. "Figured he'd get around to questioning me about her sooner or later." She nodded her head toward the hallway and her closed office door. "Let's talk in there where it's quieter."

She called out greetings to some of the guys at the bar, as she led the way to her office, with Maggie and Ace following behind.

She waited until they were seated on the sofa, then closed the door and moved behind her desk to sit down. Shifting the baby to her shoulder, she eyed Ace suspiciously. "Okay. So whaddaya wanna know?"

Ace leaned forward, bracing his forearms on his knees. "The detective I hired says Star's name wasn't really Cantrell."

Dixie lifted a shoulder, seemingly unsurprised by the news. "I figured she'd lied."

Maggie gaped. "You did? But you never said anything."

Dixie hooked a leg over her knee and settled the baby in the V she'd created between her legs.

"The girl was all smoke and mirrors. Shows up on my doorstep, carrying this beat-up suitcase and giving me this hard-luck story about a soldier she'd met in Vegas, who'd talked her into coming to Killeen. Claimed he was deployed before she ever got here, leaving her high and dry." She flapped a dismissing hand. "Hell, I've heard that story so many times, I could probably dance a tune to it."

"Are you suggesting that there was never a soldier?" Maggie asked.

Dixie shrugged. "Who knows? You couldn't pin Star

down on anything. She'd feed you a line of bull you would swear was the truth and smile the whole time you were swallowing it.''

Maggie gulped, suddenly feeling sick. ''But what about her family? Star told me they were killed in a car wreck when she was a teenager. Was that a lie, too?''

Dixie lifted a shoulder. ''Could have happened, I guess. Who knows for sure?''

''What about a social security number?'' Ace asked, redirecting the conversation to the purpose of their visit. ''Surely she had to give you some kind of legal ID, before you could hire her?''

''Oh, she had a social security card, all right,'' Dixie told him. ''I wouldn't have hired her without it.''

''And?'' he prodded.

She shrugged again. ''Probably a fake. They're easy enough to get, if you know who to ask and are willing to pay the price.''

Groaning, Ace fell back against the sofa, pressing the heels of his hands against his forehead. After a moment, he dropped his hands with a frustrated sigh. ''Without a positive ID, we might never know who she really was.''

''Any private detective worth his salt could do it,'' Dixie informed him. ''It's just a matter of turning over the right rocks and crossing the right palms.''

''I've hired the best there is,'' Ace informed her.

''Since when does a Tanner settle for anything but the best?'' she asked him, then eyed him speculatively, ''Even when the best was at home waiting on him all along.''

''Dixie!'' Maggie cried at the obvious slur.

Ace held out a hand to silence Maggie, but kept his gaze leveled on Dixie. ''I'm sure you have your reasons for saying what you did, but know this. I'm *Ace* Tanner, not Buck Tanner, and don't ever make the mistake of confusing the two.'' Rising, he crossed to the door, muttered to Maggie, "I'll be in the truck," then slammed the door behind him.

"Now don't go getting your panties in a twist," Dixie warned Maggie. She jutted her chin defensively and lifted the baby to her shoulder. "I was only testing the man's worth."

Maggie dropped her head to her hands. "Oh, Dixie," she moaned.

"Doesn't sound to me like he's changed his mind."

Still reeling from Dixie's rudeness, Maggie lifted her head. "About what?" she asked in confusion.

"The baby. He's still chasing after Star's family. That tells me he hasn't changed his mind about keeping the baby."

"Not necessarily. In fact, he's asked me to move to Kerrville with him."

"The baby, too?"

Maggie paled at the question, not having considered that Laura wouldn't be going to Kerrville with them.

Sighing, Dixie rose and rounded her desk. "Well, there's always the chance that high-priced detective of his won't find any of Star's relatives."

Maggie drew in a deep breath, grasping at that possibility. "Yeah. There's always that chance."

Placing a finger beneath Maggie's chin, Dixie drew her face up. "Prepare yourself for the worst, but pray for the best. That's what I always say."

Maggie forced a brave smile. "This is going to work out, Dix. You'll see. This is going to work just fine."

The trip home was made in silence, with Ace frowning at the road ahead and Maggie staring at the windshield, her hands fisted tightly in her lap, trying desperately to push back the doubts that Dixie had placed in her mind.

She wouldn't give up hope, she told herself. She

couldn't. Without hope, how could she survive? What would happen to Laura, if she were to give up? Who would care enough about the baby to see that she had a good home, a family to love her?

She stole a glance at Ace. She'd thought he cared, that he'd changed his mind about Laura, had grown to love her. Could she have been that wrong about him? No, she told herself. She'd seen proof of the changes over the last several weeks. Ace had warmed to Laura, bought her toys and silly little gifts. He'd even started helping Maggie with her care, feeding Laura her bottle when Maggie was busy doing something else or rocking her to sleep at night, while Maggie sat at his feet, watching, her heart nearly bursting with her love for the two of them.

She drew in a deep breath and forced her fingers apart. Ace loved Laura, she told herself firmly. He cared. This need of his to locate Star's family was probably nothing more than a formality, perhaps even a requirement he'd discovered he needed, before the courts would officially name him her legal guardian.

But she wouldn't ask him, if that was the case. Couldn't. If she did and he denied her suppositions, what would she have to place her hope in, then?

Forcing the tension from her shoulders, she reached over and laid a hand on Ace's thigh. At her touch, he glanced her way. She smiled and gave his thigh a squeeze.

"What would you like for dinner tonight?" she asked, hoping to return a sense of normalcy to what had turned into a nightmarish day.

Nine

Ever since the first night they'd made love, Maggie and Ace had slept together in his bed. It wasn't something they had discussed, an agreement they'd reached after laying down specific ground rules. It had just happened. When bedtime arrived each night, Ace would simply seek Maggie out and walk with her to his room, his arm draped along her shoulders. Often, but not always, they would make love before going to sleep, the mood of their lovemaking varying from a sweet and tender loving to hot and steamy sex.

After their visit with Dixie, they continued to sleep together…but they didn't make love any longer. Something happened that day, something intangible that left a barrier between the two that neither seemed willing to address. Yet, Ace still slept with his body curved around Maggie's, his head nestled against hers on her pillow, his feet twined with hers. He still held her hand while they watched television in the evening and dropped kisses on her mouth at moments when she least expected him to…

But he didn't make love with her again.

Though reluctant to approach Ace about the change in their relationship, Maggie worried about it, wondering at the cause, what it meant. She worried, too, about the change she noticed in his relationship with Laura. He seldom held her any more, and on those rare occasions when he did, it was because Maggie forced the baby on him. And he always seemed to disappear at Laura's bedtime, naming one task or another that required his immediate attention, thus avoiding rocking the infant to sleep.

More than the changes in her own relationship with Ace, Maggie was concerned over the changes she saw in his and Laura's. From the beginning, she'd hoped to convince him to keep Laura, raise her as his own, prayed, even, for that to happen. But with each passing day, that hope grew dimmer and dimmer, until one day it was snuffed out altogether.

The day it happened, Maggie was in the laundry room, folding a load of clothes she'd just taken from the dryer, when she heard the telephone ring. She paused, waiting to see if Ace would pick it up. After the second ring, she heard the muffled sound of Ace's voice coming from the kitchen and resumed her folding, knowing he had answered it.

"Montgomery?"

Frowning at the question Ace placed in the name, Maggie paused, listening.

"Dallas?" he said next, his voice carrying a note of surprise, then, "Damn. Here I had you chasing all over the country, when her relatives were in our own backyard the entire time."

Maggie fisted her hands in the towel she was folding, knowing it was the private detective Ace talked with.

"When you do," she heard Ace say. "Let me know. I'd think it'd be better if my brothers and I made the initial contact."

Squeezing her eyes shut, Maggie blocked out the sound of Ace's voice, not wanting to hear any more. The detective had found Star's relatives. There was no doubt about the purpose of the call. But knowing that and accepting it was a different matter altogether.

"Maggie?"

She stiffened at the sound of Ace's voice, unaware until that moment that he'd entered the laundry room and now stood behind her.

She gulped, trying to swallow back the fear that held her in its grip, her gaze fixed unseeingly on the dryer's control panel. "The detective found someone?"

"Not yet, but he knows now her name was Montgomery and he's narrowed the trail to Dallas."

Maggie dropped her chin to her chest. "You're going to give Laura to them when the detective finds them, aren't you?"

She felt the weight of his hands on her shoulders, the dig of his fingers into her flesh, as he squeezed.

"Maggie—"

She turned to face him. "Ace, please," she begged. "Don't do this. Keep her with you."

"Maggie," he said sternly, "I told you from the start that this was only a temporary arrangement."

She pressed her fists against her temples and shook her head, tears streaming down her face. "No," she cried, shaking her head. "You said you didn't know how to take care of her." She fisted her hands in his shirt and looked up at him. "But I'm here, Ace. I'll take care of her. We both can. I'm not suggesting that we get married. I know you don't want that. But we can live together, the three of us. We can give her a home, a family."

He tightened his grip on her shoulders and gave her a hard shake. "Maggie, listen to me. I don't want any kids. I told you that. Mine or anyone else's."

"No!" she screamed. She pounded her fists against his chest, desperate to make him deny his words. "You love her," she sobbed. "I know you do. You can't just give her away to a complete stranger. You can't!"

At the word *love,* he stiffened, his fingers digging painfully into her shoulders. Gulping, Maggie watched his lips flatten, his face turn to stone, his eyes turn that hard, brittle shade of steely blue she remembered from the first time they had met. She wanted to reach up and touch him, lay a hand against his cheek...but she was afraid if she dared touch him, the razor-sharp edge of the mask he'd slipped into place would slice her finger to the bone.

Frightened by the change in him, devastated by it, she backed away from him, hugging her arms around her middle, as if to ward off a chill.

"I won't stand by and watch you give her away," she told him. "I...I can't." Choked by a sob, she spun and ran from the room.

Maggie folded the soggy tissue and blotted at the tears that continued to stream down her face. "I can't believe he's really going to do it, Dixie."

Dixie plucked a fresh tissue from the box and pressed it into Maggie's hand, her face creased with concern. "Ah, honey. I know it hurts. It's gotta. But there's nothin' you can do to stop him. By law, Ace can do what he wants to with the child."

Maggie shot up from the couch. "Law," she repeated, venom all but dripping from her lips at the word. "I'm sick to death of people using *law* as an excuse for their behavior. What about duty? Huh? What about love? Why doesn't anyone ever base their actions on either of those things? Why do they always have to fall back on what the *law* says? Why can't they listen to what their hearts say, instead?"

Dixie caught Maggie's hand and pulled her back down on the sofa beside her. "Now, Maggie," she scolded gently. "You're just getting yourself all worked up again, when what you need to do is calm down."

Maggie balled her hands against her thighs. "But I'm so mad, Dixie. Furious! Every time I think about Ace giving that precious baby away, I want to hit something. Him! How can he be so blind that he can't see that he loves her? So heartless that he can't see that she needs him?"

Dixie patted her knee. "Now, honey, I know that you think you know what's best for the child. But are you sure you aren't the one who's having difficulty seeing? You forged a bond with that baby the minute Star placed her in your arms. But does that give you the right to dictate the child's future? To decide what's best for her and what's not? Star asked you to take her to the Tanners and that's what you did.

"Maybe you need to open up your own eyes and see what's really behind this anger of yours. You've been living out on that ranch with Ace, for what? Close to a month? I'd imagine, by now, you're sleeping with him."

Dixie didn't need confirmation from Maggie to know she was right. The stricken look on Maggie's face was enough. Sighing, she gave Maggie's knee an understanding squeeze. "I figured as much."

"I love him."

Frowning, Dixie nodded. "I don't doubt that for a minute. You'd never have crawled into bed with him, if you didn't. But what about him? How does he feel about you?"

Maggie balled the tissue in her hand and rubbed a thumb at the fist she'd made. "I don't know. I thought he did…or at least that he cared." She turned to look at Dixie, tears filling her eyes. "He wouldn't have asked me to move to Kerrville with him, if he didn't care for me, would he?"

"Only Ace can answer that. He's the one who knows

his heart. But I imagine once he suggested you move in with him, you started fancying yourself a family. Mama Bear. Papa Bear. Baby Bear. A big, fine home for the three of you to live in.'' She lifted a brow. ''Am I right?''

Maggie stared, amazed at how accurately Dixie had depicted the sequence of her emotions, her thoughts.

Dixie reared back to look at her. ''What? You think you're the first woman to let her dreams run away with her?'' She shook her head sadly. ''Honey, if I was to stand up behind you all the women who'd made that same mistake, the line would stretch for miles.''

''Knowing that doesn't lessen the hurt.''

''I doubt it does. But this isn't the end of the world, so don't you start acting like it is. You've hit a little rough spot, taken a spill. But you'll survive. That's what we women do. We survive.''

Gulping back tears, Maggie leaned to rest her head against Dixie's. ''Oh, Dix. What would I do without you?''

Dixie wrapped an arm around her and gave her a hard squeeze. ''Oh, you'd do all right. You've got a good head on your shoulders. A good heart. You'd find your way.''

Sniffing, Maggie blew her nose. ''Eventually, I guess.'' She angled her head to look at Dixie. ''You know, Dix,'' she said thoughtfully. ''It's a shame you never had children. You'd have made a wonderful mother.''

Dixie snorted a laugh. ''You're just saying that to butter me up. Probably want your old job back.''

Chuckling, Maggie blotted the last tears from her eyes. ''No, but I'd sure like to have it, if it's still available.''

Dixie pursed her lips, as if considering. ''I suppose by now you've forgotten all I taught you. How to tote a loaded tray without strainin' your back. How to dodge a strayin' hand without insultin' the man whose hand did the strayin'.''

Laughing, Maggie hugged Dixie against her side. "No. I haven't forgotten."

"Then I suppose you're back on the payroll."

Dixie stood at the rear entrance of the Longhorn, watching as Maggie climbed into that rag-tail car of hers. She'd been tough on the girl, she thought with regret. But Maggie had needed a good shaking up, to jar her out of the doldrums before they swallowed her all the way up.

It hadn't been easy for Dixie to give her that shaking, though. Not when what she'd wanted to do was wrap her arms around the child and soak up all her pain. But Dixie had discovered long ago that you couldn't spare another from hurt, no matter how badly you wanted to or how hard you tried. Sometimes you just had to sit back and watch 'em take the fall. Oh, you could pick 'em up and dust off their knees, afterwards. Slap a bandage on the hurt. But you couldn't spare them the pain. Life had a way of getting in its blows no matter how good you got at duckin' and dodgin' 'em.

Star was to blame for all this, Dixie thought, trying to stifle the resentment that came with the thought. Saddling Maggie with the responsibility of her baby. Another person would've delivered the kid, as Star had requested, then walked away and wiped her hands of the matter. Not Maggie. She'd taken on the responsibility as if it was her life's work and now suffered a tremendous guilt because she thought she'd failed.

But if anybody understood that kind of dedication, Dixie supposed she did. She'd made a similar promise a few years back, one she still felt bound by today.

She'd made the promise to Patricia Dean.

Maggie's mother.

Ace sat slumped over the kitchen table, his chin resting on its edge, a bottle of whiskey between his hands, turning it slowly around and around, while he tried to work up the enthusiasm to pour himself a drink. It wasn't his brand. Not that he had a favorite. The truth was, he'd never particularly cared for the taste of whiskey.

But he did have a hankering for the escape it promised.

Scowling, he shoved the bottle away and flopped back in his chair.

Hell, he couldn't get drunk. Not with a baby in the house and him the only adult around to take care of it.

But remembering that didn't take away his hankering for escape. It only served to remind him that Maggie was gone.

Slumping lower in the chair, he folded his arms across his chest, his anger with her returning. Packing up her stuff and tearing out like the devil himself was chasing her. What the hell was wrong with her? It wasn't as if he'd lied about his intentions. He'd told her from the get-go that he wasn't keeping the kid. So why had she turned on the waterworks and begged him to keep her?

Frustrated that he didn't have an answer to the question, he heaved himself up from the chair. "Women," he muttered.

At the sink, he twisted on the tap and sent hot water splashing over the bottles and nipples he'd left in the sink. Maggie should be doing this, he thought, as he squirted a generous stream of dishwashing liquid over the bottles. She'd always washed and prepared the baby's bottles for the next day. Not him. And she'd done a lot of other things that now fell to him. Things like feeding the baby, playing with her, giving her her baths.

The hell of it was, he didn't begrudge Maggie the work she'd left him to do. What he resented was that she'd left at all.

Daisy barked at a sound in the hall, startling Ace from his thoughts. He whirled, sure it was Maggie returning, figuring that she'd realized she'd made a mistake. That she'd finally reconciled herself to the fact that Ace was turning the baby over to Star's family.

When it was Rory who appeared in the doorway, not Maggie, Ace turned back to the sink to hide his disappointment.

Snatching up a bottle scrubber, he growled, "What do you want?"

"A man has to have a reason to visit his family home?"

Ace rammed the brush into the bottle and scrubbed furiously. "Funny to me, you never cared about visiting until Maggie showed up."

"So *that's* what's been eating you."

Ace rammed the brush hard into the bottle, then swore when it busted through the opposite end, sending shards of glass flying over both sinks.

"Now look what you've gone and made me do," he complained.

"I didn't make you do anything."

"You damn sure did. You made me break the bottle."

Rory moved to Ace's side and looked down at the shattered glass. "I didn't make you do that. Your jealousy did."

"Jealousy!" Ace cried. "And who am I supposed to be jealous of? You?" He snorted a breath. "In your dreams, little brother. In your dreams."

"Then explain to me why you acted like an ass the night I took you to the emergency room to have your ribs X-rayed?"

Ace tensed. He didn't remember much of anything that happened that night...not after about the fourth glass of whiskey he'd drunk. Had he said something to Rory about Maggie? He remembered Maggie telling him the next morning that he owed Rory an apology for cussing Rory when he'd helped him to bed. But what had he said to Rory at the emergency room?

Deciding a defensive stance the safest to take, he said, "Probably because you provoked me."

"Which proves my point."

"And what point is *that?*"

Smiling smugly, Rory braced a hip on the counter and folded his arms across his chest. "You're jealous."

Ace yanked his hands from the dishwater and snatched up a towel to dry them. "What would you have that I'd be jealous of?"

Rory curled his fingers to study his nails. "It's not what I have. More like what you're afraid I might get."

Ace turned for the table and the whiskey bottle he'd left there. Twisting off the cap, he arched a brow in warning, as he lifted the bottle to his lips. "You try stealing my dog, little brother, and I'll kick your butt all the way to Dallas and back."

"It wasn't your dog I was thinking of stealing. I was thinking more along the lines of Maggie."

Ace slammed down the bottle, without ever having taken a drink, and leveled an accusing finger at Rory. "I knew it!" he cried. "I *knew* you had the hots for her all along."

When Rory only smiled, it angered Ace all the more. He dug down in his arsenal and selected a weapon sure to draw blood.

"What's wrong, Rory?" he taunted. "Aren't there enough women in San Antonio to satisfy your sexual appetite? Or have you grown bored with them all?" Snorting a laugh, Ace turned away. "You're so much like the old man, it's scary."

"Why, you—"

Rory was across the room, before Ace knew he'd even moved. Grabbing Ace by the arm, he spun him around.

"You've been lookin' for a fight for weeks," he said

angrily and gave Ace a shove. "Well, bro, you just found yourself one."

Ace squared off, ready to go head-to-head with Rory, but a wail from the monitor he'd left on the table had him dropping his hands.

"Now look what you've done," he snapped. "You woke up the kid."

Rory took a taunting jab at Ace's shoulder. "Let Maggie get her. You and me are going to settle this once and for all."

Ace turned away, heading for the hallway. "Maggie's gone."

Rory slowly lowered his hands to stare. "Gone?"

When Ace kept walking, Rory took off after him. "What do you mean she's gone?"

"As in vamoosed. Skedaddled."

"Where'd she go?"

"Back where she came from."

Opening the nursery door, Ace reached to turn on the lamp, then moved to the crib.

"Hey, kid," he murmured softly, as he leaned to pick Laura up. "What's the matter? Huh? You hungry?"

"Hungry?" Rory repeated. "Haven't you fed her?"

Ace gave him a withering look. "Well, of course I've fed her. What do you take me for? An imbecile?"

Rory lifted a shoulder. "Well, you let Maggie go."

Scowling, Ace moved to the changing table and laid the baby down. "I didn't *let* Maggie do anything. She got mad and quit."

"Mad about what?"

Wishing he'd kept his mouth shut, Ace gestured for Rory to pass him a diaper. "The detective thinks he's close to finding a relative of Star's."

Rory handed him the diaper. "Why'd that make her

mad? I'd think she'd be tinkled pink, Star being her friend and all."

Frowning, Ace held up the baby's feet, doused her behind with some powder, then lowered them to snug the diaper into place. "She wanted me to keep the kid."

"You?" Rory hooted a laugh. "Is the woman crazy? You don't know anything about raising kids."

Ace turned his head and gave him a long look up and down. "You look like you survived the experience without too many scars."

"Well, yeah," Rory said. "But I'm a guy. I was easy."

"Easy?" Ace snorted and picked the baby up. "You were a royal pain in the butt. All of you were."

With the baby draped over his shoulder, Ace headed for the door, leaving Rory to trail behind.

"Is that why you never wanted to have kids?" Rory asked.

Ace slammed to a stop, then turned to look at Rory. "Who told you I never wanted to have kids?"

"Sheila."

"When did you talk to my ex?"

Rory held up his hands. "Uh-uh. I'm not walking into that one. Next thing I know, you'll be accusing me of hustling your ex-wife."

Scowling, Ace headed for the kitchen again. "Like she'd be interested in you."

"Is that what busted up your marriage?"

"You? Hardly."

"No," Rory said in frustration. "You not wanting any kids."

Ace pulled a bottle from the refrigerator and popped it into the microwave, set the timer. "Among other things."

Hooking his thumbs through his belt loops, Rory hung his head. "Man, Ace. I feel really bad."

"About what?"

"Ruining you for fatherhood. If not for me and the others, you might've had kids."

"You didn't ruin me for anything," he told Rory, then added, "well, not entirely, anyway."

"If not us, then what did? Sheila said you were emphatic about not wanting any kids. Said you'd even talked about having a vasectomy."

"Did she discuss our sex life with you, too?"

The microwave dinged, saving Rory from having to answer. Holding the baby against his shoulder, Ace removed the bottle and tested the milk's temperature on his wrist, as he moved to sit at the table.

Noticing Rory's hangdog expression, Ace heaved a sigh. "Look, Rory. Sheila and I had problems before the question of kids ever came up. That's not what ended our marriage."

Rory twirled a chair around and straddled it. "I don't get it, Ace. Why don't you want to have kids?"

Ace looked down at Laura and shook his head. "I don't know. A combination of things, I guess. Mostly the old man." He frowned, then glanced over at Rory. "Haven't you ever wondered what kind of father you'd be? A good one or a bad one? Or like the old man? Invisible?"

Rory pursed his lips thoughtfully, as if considering. "No, I can't say that I have."

Ace blew out a long breath. "Well, I have. And there's enough doubt there to keep me from testing the theory."

Rory reared back to look at him in disbelief. "You gotta be kidding me! You'd make a great father, Ace."

"Yeah. Right," Ace said wryly.

Rory pushed up from the chair. "No. I'm serious. Ask Woodrow or Ry or even Whit. They'd tell you the same damn thing. I know we were pains in the butt and acted like ungrateful jerks most of the time. What kid doesn't?

But you were there for us, Ace. When we needed you, you never let us down.

"We may have resented you bossing us around, but we would've resented you for that even if you'd been our real father and not just a stand-in. And just look at you," Rory said, gesturing toward Ace and the baby. "You're taking care of her. You've got what it takes to be a father. You're a natural."

As Ace stared down at the baby, Maggie's words rose up to taunt him.

No child deserves to have a father who's incapable of loving or caring for it.

Was he incapable of loving the kid? he asked himself. Unsure of the answer, he shook his head. "No. I can do the basics. Meet a kid's physical needs. But that's it. A kid need someone who can love 'em and that's where I come up short."

"Like hell you do!" Rory shouted. "Who held my hand when I had to have my stomach pumped, after I swallowed an entire bottle of headache pills?"

Ace snorted a laugh, remembering. "I did."

"And who taught me how to ride a horse and rope a steer?"

"I did. But—"

"And who let me crawl in bed with him in the middle of the night, when a storm blew in and I was too scared to sleep in my own bed?"

Grimacing, Ace muttered. "I did."

Rory dropped a hand on Ace's shoulder and hunkered down to look him square in the eye. "If those weren't acts of love, bro, then you tell me what is."

Ace lay on his side, his head propped on his hand, staring down at the baby who slept beside him. This was the fourth

night in a row that he'd had to put the baby in bed with
him in order to get her to go to sleep.

Maggie had warned him, he remembered. She'd told him
he was starting a bad habit when he'd put the baby in bed
with them that first time.

But how the hell was a man supposed to get any rest
with the kid screaming her lungs out?

Screaming her lungs out? his conscience prodded.

Well, maybe not screaming, he acceded grudgingly.
Probably more like crying.

Crying?

Okay, already! he thought in frustration. So it was a
whimper. But what was I supposed to do? The kid was
lonely in that big old room all by herself.

Who was lonely?

Groaning, he dropped his hand and let his head fall to
rest in the bend of his elbow. Me, he admitted miserably.

"But I'm not the only one who's lonely," he murmured.
Reaching out, he brushed a finger over the baby's cheek.
"You miss her, too, don't you, kid?"

At his touch, Laura shuddered a sigh, then smacked her
lips, as if searching for the missing pacifier.

Ace plucked the pacifier from the pillow he'd propped
up on the other side of the baby and rubbed the nipple
across her lips. She latched onto it, sucked furiously for a
moment, then her jaw went lax and the pacifier slid to dan-
gle from the corner of her mouth. It was a game they repeated several times a night. The baby makes a sucking
sound; Ace fetches the pacifier; the baby sucks a minute,
quits; the pacifier falls out of the baby's mouth; the baby
makes another sucking sound, sometimes a whimper; and
the game starts all over again.

Ace felt something cold nudge the back of his leg and
looked over his shoulder to find Daisy staring up at him.

"No way," he said. "I may be a sucker, but I'll be darned if I'll let you sleep with me, too."

The dog dropped her chin to the edge of the mattress and whined pitifully, looking up at him with sad brown eyes.

Swearing under his breath, Ace patted the bed. "All right, you big baby. Get up here."

Daisy bounded onto the bed, then flopped down at Ace's feet.

"And stay there," he warned the dog. "I don't want you waking up the kid."

Catching the end of the sheet, Ace pulled it up over his shoulder and settled his head onto his pillow, closed his eyes.

But even with all the company, sleep was still a long time coming for Ace.

It was Maggie he wanted with him in his bed.

Ten

Ace awakened slowly. Blinked, then flipped his eyes wide. Jackknifing up, he looked frantically around. The baby was gone. The dog was gone. Whipping back the sheet, he vaulted from the bed and ran from his room.

At the doorway to the kitchen, he skidded to a stop. Rory sat at the table, calmly feeding the baby a bottle, the dog sprawled at his feet. Bracing a hand on the jamb, Ace placed the other over his heart to still its wild beating.

Rory shot him a grin. "Mornin', Ace."

Ace sank weakly down onto a chair and dropped his head into his hands. "Damn you, Rory. You nearly gave me a heart attack."

Rory bit back a smile. "Why? Did you think somebody had kidnaped the kid?"

Ace lifted his head to scowl. "Hell, I didn't know what to think." He snatched up a dish towel from the table and used one corner to catch a milky drop of drool that leaked from the side of the baby's mouth. "Scared the pee-waddly-doo out of me, though, and that's a damn fact."

Rory gave him a disapproving look. "You probably shouldn't cuss like that in front of the kid." He looked down at the baby and smiled. "A pretty little thing like her? It'd be a shame if the first word out of her mouth was a four-letter one."

Ace snorted a breath. "By the time she starts talking, I won't be around to influence her, good or bad."

Rory glanced up at Ace. "Are you sure you want to turn her over to Star's relatives? I mean, think about it, Ace. You don't know anything about these people. They could be ex-cons, for all you know."

Ace pushed away from the table. "And they might be good, law-abiding folks," he argued stubbornly, as he headed for the sink.

"What about Maggie?" Rory asked. "Why doesn't she adopt her?"

The question hit Ace square in the back, stabbing so deep it pierced his heart, releasing a memory he'd buried there. Though his gaze was fixed on the window above the sink, it wasn't the view of the backyard he saw beyond the glass. It was Maggie he saw. Standing on the front porch the day she'd brought the baby to the ranch, her face ravaged with regret, her eyes swollen with tears, her voice trembling as she'd told him she'd wanted to keep the baby herself, but couldn't.

She deserves more than I can give her.

He shook his head, not trusting his voice. "She can't."

"Why not? It's obvious she's crazy about the kid."

Ace squeezed his eyes shut, trying to shut out the images that flashed through his mind. Images of Maggie holding the baby, rocking her. The love that filled her eyes each time she looked at the child.

Gulping, he forced open his eyes to stare blindly at the

window. "Maggie wants her to have a family. One that will love her and take care of her."

"You could do that, Ace. You and Maggie together could give the kid that."

Ace shook his head. "Maggie could. But not me."

"That's bull, Ace, and you know it. You love Maggie, don't you?"

Ace gripped his hands over the sink, as the reality of that hit him. He hadn't intended to fall in love with her. Couldn't even remember at what point his feelings had changed, grown into something stronger.

"Don't go trying to deny it," Rory warned, "because I know better. Twice you wanted to fight me because I flirted with her. In my book, that spells jealousy with a capital J. And, if you're jealous, that means you've staked a claim on her, which is fine with me, 'cause I like Maggie and wouldn't mind having her for a sister-in-law."

Ace gulped. "Maggie doesn't want to get married. She told me so."

"Well, she either lied or changed her mind, because last night she told me that she did and was willing to marry you."

Ace's heart stuttered a beat. Slowly he turned to stare at Rory. "You saw Maggie?"

"I damn sure did and it wasn't to flirt with her, so don't go swelling up like a bullfrog and trying to pick a fight with me again. I went to talk to her, to try to figure out what the hell was going on between the two of you."

Ace pressed his hands to his head to still the dizzying sensation, trying to absorb what Rory was saying. "She told you that she loved me?"

"Not right off. I had to fish a little first."

"She never said anything," he said dully. "Never told me how she felt."

"Did you tell her?"

Regret burned through Ace that he hadn't, that it had taken losing her to make him realize that he did.

Rory shook his head sadly. "Bro, you may be older, but you sure as hell aren't wiser. Not where women are concerned. Maybe I should give you a couple of pointers."

Ace started for the door. "Stay with the baby. I'll be back as quick as I can."

"Hey!" Rory cried. "Where are you going?"

Ace twisted open the door and started out. "To get Maggie."

"Wait!" Rory shouted.

Ace stopped and looked back. "What?" he snapped in frustration.

"You might want to put on some pants first."

Ace looked down and groaned when he realized that he was wearing nothing but his shorts. Closing the door, he ran for his room.

"Watch out for Dixie," Rory called after him. "Judging by the fuss she kicked up last night when Maggie told her I was your brother, I figure you're probably pretty high on her hit list right now."

When Ace didn't find Maggie at home, he drove straight to the Longhorn, figuring he'd find her there. Sure enough, he spotted her beat-up car in the parking lot beside the building. Parking his truck next to it, he climbed out and headed for the front entrance. He tried the door but found it locked. Framing his hands at his temples, he pressed his face against the glass, trying to see inside. The place looked empty, but he'd swear he heard music.

Lifting a fist, he pounded on the door. "Maggie?" he shouted. "It's me. Ace. Open the door."

He waited a moment, listening, then lifted his hand to pound again. Just as he did, the door opened and Dixie stepped out.

She narrowed her eyes at the fist he managed to halt short inches from her nose.

"Hit me," she snarled, "and I'll have the cops on you so fast it'll make your head spin."

Ace dropped his hand. "I'm not planning on hitting anyone. I want to see Maggie."

"And why would she want to see you?"

By the bitterness in the woman's voice, Ace figured Rory had been right. He was pretty high on Dixie's hit list. Probably on Maggie's, too.

"I don't know that she does," he told her, trying to keep the frustration from his voice. "But I'd appreciate it if you'd tell her that I'm here."

"And why would I want to do that?" Dixie challenged. "Appears to me you've hurt her enough as it is."

At the end of his patience, Ace closed his hands around Dixie's arms and bodily picked her up. He stepped through the doorway, then kicked the door closed behind him.

"Now," he said and plopped her back down on her feet. "You can either tell me where Maggie is, or I can tear this place apart looking for her. Either way, I'm not leaving until I talk to her."

Dixie aimed a finger at his nose. "You hurt that girl again and you'll have me to deal with. Understand?"

Ace caught her hand, pulled it down and pushed his face up to hers. "Perfectly. Now you understand something. I love Maggie and I intend to marry her, if she'll have me, so you better learn to deal with that *and* me, because I'm not going away. Ever. Understand?"

"Ace...what are you doing here?"

He whipped around to find Maggie standing behind the bar. All he could do was stare.

A slap on the back had him stumbling forward a step.

"Well, you said you wanted to talk to her," Dixie snapped. "So? There she is. Talk."

Ace angled his head around to give Dixie a murderous look. "In private, if you don't mind," he grated out between clenched teeth.

Dixie tossed up her hands. "Well, why didn't you say you wanted privacy, 'stead of standing there staring at the girl like a mute."

Muttering under her breath, she stalked to the back hallway and slammed her office door behind her. "Okay!" she shouted from behind the closed door. "I'm in my office now! That's as private as you're gonna get, so talk!"

"Ace?"

Taking a deep breath, he turned back to face Maggie. But, at the sight, his throat closed up around the words he'd come to say to her. He walked slowly toward the bar, braced a hand on its top and vaulted over. With his gaze on hers, he took her hands in his and brought them to his lips. He watched the tears fill her eyes, felt the burn of them behind his own.

"You said you wanted Laura to have a family who loved and cared for her."

She squeezed her eyes shut, dipped her head. Nodded.

"I think I've found the perfect family for her."

Her desolation was obvious, evidenced by the droop of her shoulders, the lifeless relaxing of her hands within his, the tear that leaked past one lid to trail slowly down her cheek.

"They'll be good to her," he promised. "Good for her. They'll give her everything she needs, everything she could ever possibly want."

A sob slipped past her lips and she tried to wrench her hands free.

But Ace hung on, refusing to let her go.

"It's what you wanted, isn't it?" he asked quietly. "A home for Laura, a family to love her?"

She lifted her head, her eyes flooded with tears. "Yes,

that's what I wanted," she cried tearfully. "But I wanted *you* to be the one to provide that home for her, *you* to be the one to love her." Hiccuping a sob, she jerked her hands free and dropped her face onto her palms. "Not just anyone, Ace," she sobbed. "I wanted it to be you."

"I can't do that, Maggie," he said softly. "Not alone. Not without you. Maggie...." He pulled her hands from her face to hold in his. "Marry me, Maggie. Help me create that home for Laura. Help me remember how to love."

She gulped, staring. "Oh, Ace..." She gulped again. Swallowed. "Do you mean it? You're really going to keep her?"

He guided her arms around him, then wrapped his around her. "That's my plan." Reaching up, he thumbed a tear from her cheek. "But Star has family. We know that now. They may want Laura, too."

He felt the dig of her fingers on his back, saw the fear that flashed in her eyes, and wanted desperately to reassure her. "I don't know what the laws are," he told her. "Whose rights for guardianship prevail in a situation like this. But I promise you this. I will do everything within my power to see that Laura remains with us."

She sagged against him, clutching him to her. "Oh, Ace," she cried softly. "She has to. She just has to."

He held her close, slowly rocking her back and forth, his lips pressed against the side of her head. "I love you, Maggie," he whispered. "More than I even dreamed possible."

She leaned back to look up at him, her eyes filled with tears. "And I love you, Ace."

"Marry me, Maggie." He thumbed a tear from her cheek, then dropped his mouth to hers. "Marry me and we'll work through this together, start building on that home you want for Laura."

Smiling through her tears, she framed his face with her hands. "Yes. Together. Oh, Ace..." She flung her arms around him, hugging him tight. "This is going to turn out all right. I just know it will."

"It will, Maggie. The three of us belong together. We're family."

Epilogue

It was almost two months to the day from their father's funeral that the four Tanner brothers gathered in their father's office again. As they had during that first meeting, Woodrow and Rory sat on the leather sofa opposite their father's desk. Ry stood to the left of the desk, his arms folded across his chest, frowning out the window.

In addition to the four brothers, two others were present for this meeting. Whit, who had missed the first meeting, stood on the far side of the room next to the door, his back braced against the wall. Maggie, the newest addition to the Tanner family, was present, as well, and stood at her husband Ace's side, before the desk.

A third person was present, as well. Laura was there and currently being passed from brother-to-brother and—according to Ace—at risk of becoming terminally spoiled.

When the baby finally made it back to Maggie, Ace draped an arm along Maggie's shoulder, and addressed his brothers.

"I think all of you are aware that the private detective I hired has discovered that Star's real name was Montgomery, not Cantrell, and that he's traced her family to Dallas."

Receiving nods of affirmation from his brothers, Ace went on. "Well, now it looks as if he's located a family member. Specifically, a sister."

Rory shot from the sofa, his eyes wide in alarm. "But you and Maggie are keepin' the baby, right? This sister can't take Laura away from us, can she?"

His expression grim, Ace shook his head. "I don't know. That's what we've got to find out. None of the lawyers we have on retainer practice family law, so they're having to research the laws pertaining to guardianship and custodial rights, in situations where both parents die, leaving a child behind. Since neither Star nor the old man left behind a will or specific written instructions pertaining to Laura's welfare, for now we are going to have to assume that Star's sister has the same rights to Laura as any of us do."

Rory dropped weakly back down on the sofa. "Then what?" he asked, lifting his hands helplessly. "I mean, if this sister wants Laura, who decides who gets to keep her?"

Releasing a long breath, Ace withdrew his arm from Maggie and hitched a hip on the corner of the desk. "I guess the courts will."

"Oh, man," Rory moaned. "That could get ugly."

"I'm hoping to avoid that," Ace informed him.

"How?" Rory asked, clearly puzzled as to how they could circumvent a court ruling.

Ace pushed off the desk and began to pace. "As far as we know, this sister doesn't even know Laura exists. My plan is to get to her as quickly as we can, explain the situation to her, then hopefully persuade her to let Maggie and I adopt the baby."

Rory flapped his hands, as if urging them out the door. "So go! The sooner we get this settled, the better, as far as I'm concerned. I know, I for one, will sleep a hell of a lot better once the kid's name is officially Tanner.''

''Maggie and I have discussed this,'' Ace told him, ''and we both agree that we shouldn't be the ones to make the initial contact.''

Ry glanced over his shoulder to look at Ace. ''Are you sending one of our lawyers?''

Ace shook his head. ''No. I think it would be better if a member of the family met with her.'' He glanced at Rory. ''What about you? You're personable, yet I know you can be pretty damn persuasive when it suits you. Would you be willing to do it?''

''Oh, man, Ace,'' Rory said miserably. ''You know I'd do it in a heartbeat. But I'm leaving tonight for Wyoming. I've got meetings scheduled all week with a group of Western artists whose work I want to carry in my store. If you could give me a couple of days—''

''No,'' Ace said, frowning. ''A couple of days is too long to wait.'' He turned to Ry. ''What about you? Do you think you could squeeze a trip to Dallas into your schedule?''

''Sorry,'' Ry said. ''The funeral and my trips here to help out on the ranch have thrown me way behind. I have surgeries scheduled back to back all day, starting at six in the morning. My whole week's like that.''

''What about you, Whit?'' Ace asked, shifting his gaze to the back of the room where Whit stood.

Whit paled. ''Not me, Ace, please. I wouldn't know what to say. What to do.''

''I think Woodrow should be the one to go.''

Four heads spun to stare at Maggie in disbelief.

Woodrow made a choking sound. ''Me?'' he croaked.

Maggie gave her chin a decisive nod. ''You're the perfect choice.''

''But I hate big cities!'' When Maggie merely lifted a

brow, he looked around the room, desperately searching for support. Finding none, he appealed to Ace. "Come on, Ace. You know what my negotiating skills are like. It's my way or the highway."

Ace felt a bump against his arm and turned, taking the baby Maggie pushed into his arms. Wondering what she was up to, he watched her cross to Woodrow and sink down at his feet.

"You can do it, Woodrow," she said confidently. "I wouldn't allow you to represent us if I didn't think you were capable of handling the job."

He drew back, shaking his head slowly. "You don't know me like the rest of 'em do. I don't deal well with people."

She laid a hand on his knee. "You love Laura, don't you?"

"Ah, Maggie," he complained. "That's fightin' dirty. You know I'm crazy about the kid."

"Yes, and because you love her, I know you will fight as hard to keep her as Ace or I would. Will you do this for us? Please? For Laura?"

He glanced over at the baby, gulped, then dropped his chin to his chest, his shoulders sagging in defeat. "All right," he grumbled, then lifted his head to narrow an eye at Maggie. "But if I screw this up, I don't want anyone blamin' me. Understood?"

Laughing, Maggie rose to throw her arms around his neck. "You won't screw this up, Woodrow. You're the perfect man for the job."

Late that same night, Maggie and Ace lay in bed, the lights out, but both wide awake.

"He *could* screw this up," Ace said for the umpteenth time since his brothers had left. "Woodrow's people skills are a little rough around the edges."

Maggie laced her fingers through Ace's. "He won't," she said confidently.

"But he could, you know. To folks that don't know him, Woodrow comes across as abrasive."

"Yes," she agreed. "His size alone is intimidating. One look at him, and Star's poor sister will probably run and hide."

"Oh, God," Ace moaned. "Maybe I should call and tell him to forget it."

When he leaned to reach for the phone, Maggie tightened her grip on his hand. "Don't you dare," she warned, then softened the scolding with a smile, as he laid back down beside her. "Woodrow will do just fine," she assured him. "You'll see. He loves Laura as much as we do."

Pulling his hand from hers, Ace slid it beneath her shoulders and pulled her to his side. "You're right," he said, hugging her close. "All my brothers are crazy about the kid. Not just Woodrow."

She laid her head on his shoulder. "Everything's going to work out all right, Ace. Laura was meant to be with us. I feel it in my heart."

He turned his lips to her forehead. "You'll make a wonderful mother, Maggie. And I want to be a good father to her. Better than my father was to me."

She lifted a hand to cup his cheek, emotion filling her throat. "You already are, Ace. You love her. That's what's most important."

Covering her hand with his, he smiled down at her. "I'm one lucky man to have you as my wife. I love you more than I ever thought was possible."

"And I love you, Ace."

He snuggled close and bumped his nose against hers. "How do you feel about giving Laura a couple of brothers or sisters?"

"Oh, Ace," she said tearfully. "I think that would be wonderful!"

He pressed his lips to hers. "Think we ought to start working on that now?"

She drew back to look at him in surprise. "Now?"

He shrugged. "If we don't hurry up and get another baby for those brothers of mine to spoil, they're going to ruin Laura for sure."

Laughing, she looped her arms behind his neck. "In that case, I guess we better not waste any more time."

* * * * *

One

"If you'd rather be alone," she said quickly, "I can go back inside."

Frowning, Woodrow shook his head and turned to look out at his land again. "I wasn't doing anything but enjoying the view. There's plenty enough for two."

He heard the soft pad of her feet on the wooden planks of the porch behind him and dropped his hands between his knees to hide his arousal. As she sank down beside him, the hem of her dress brushed his thigh, an unintentional caress that had him swallowing a groan.

Her gaze on the horizon, she pulled her knees up and tucked the hem of her dress over her bare feet. A soft smile curved her lips. "It's beautiful."

He followed the line of her gaze to the sunset. "Yeah," he agreed. "It is that."

"It sounds ridiculous, I know, but we don't see sunsets like this in the city. At least, not where I live."

He nodded, understanding what she meant. "Cities have too many buildings for a person to see much of anything. And all those lights?" He shook his head and gestured toward the reds, pinks and golds emblazoned on the horizon. "The illumination from 'em diminishes the sunset's colors. Makes 'em look all washed out."

She tilted her head, as if considering his explanation. "I never thought of it that way before," she said thoughtfully, then glanced over at him and smiled. "But you're right. The colors are bolder here, more vibrant."

He knew that she had spoken, but couldn't have repeated her words if someone had put a gun to his head and demanded he do so. The moment she'd smiled, it was as if something had wrapped itself around his chest and squeezed, her smile's effect on him was that strong. It transformed her face, illuminated her eyes.

Her eyes, he thought, noticing for the first time how beautiful they were. Why hadn't he noticed them before? Maybe because, tonight, she wasn't wearing her glasses. Without the distracting frames and lenses, he saw that her eyes were almond-shaped and framed by long, thick lashes. Though blue like his, the irises in her were shades lighter, making them appear softer. Kinder. Looking into them was like peering into a deep pool that reflected her soul. Every emotion she felt was there for him to see, every shadow on her heart exposed.

As he stared, tongue-tied by the beauty of her eyes and the secrets they held, a cloud of uncertainty swept over them.

She lifted a hand to her cheek. "Do I have something on my face?"

He shook his head, but it took a moment for him to find his voice. "No. There's nothing wrong with your face." When she continued to hold her hand there self-consciously, he caught it and drew it down. "Your face is perfect. I promise."

Her blush was the shade of innocence and touched his heart in a way nothing had in a long time. He should have released her hand then. Instead, he found himself lacing his fingers through hers and drawing it to rest with his on his thigh. She didn't attempt to pull away, but he felt the tremble of her fingers within his and wondered at it.

She was a mature woman. Having a man hold her hand shouldn't spook her. Was it *him* who made her uneasy? he wondered. Or was her uneasiness due to something else?

Like a man back in Dallas.

He swore silently, not having considered the possibility.

He curled his fingers tighter around hers, determined to find out. "Doc, I know there's probably a more delicate way of asking this, but damned if I know what it is." He inhaled a bracing breath, then asked in a rush, "Has someone staked a claim on you?"

She blinked at him in confusion. "What?"

"Do you have a boyfriend?" he asked impatiently.

"There was," she said quietly, then sighed and met his gaze. "But not any longer."

Relief washed though him in waves. Pushing off the porch, he stood and drew her up to stand opposite him. "Good. Because I sure wouldn't want someone to come gunning for me."

She sputtered a laugh. "Why would anyone come—"

Before she could finish the question, he slipped his arms around her waist and pulled her hips to his. As he lowered his face over hers, he saw the surprise that flared in her eyes, a split second before he touched his lips to hers.

He didn't thrust his tongue down her throat or rip off her dress...though he had a powerful urge to do both. Instead, he keep the kiss light, the pressure of his mouth on hers non-threatening. It was the right thing to do. He knew it the moment he felt the soft melting of her body against his, the slow parting of her lips beneath his. Only then did he dare deepen the kiss.

She tasted so sweet, so innocent. Felt so incredibly *right* in his arms. Soft. Utterly feminine…and totally naked beneath the gauzy dress. He first suspected this when her breasts flattened beneath his chest's urging. He knew it for a fact when his hands encountered no bra straps or elastic panty bands on their downward path to her hips.

Cupping her low, he lifted her, holding her against him, and groaned as the hard ridge of her pelvic bone grazed his arousal.

His blood pumped hot through his veins, his pulse roared in his ears. He was taking things too fast. Too far. Not for him. But for her. The doc was fragile, both emotionally and physically. To take her to bed and make love with her now would be taking advantage of her weakened emotional state, something he feared she'd regret. If not by morning, eventually.

Lowering her slowly back to her feet, he framed a hand at her face and slowly forced her head back so he could look at her. Her face remained tipped up to his, her eyes shuttered close, her lips moist and slightly parted. He felt the thrum of her pulse in the arms wound around his neck, the warmth of her breath against his chin. As he stared, mesmerized by her beauty, her lids lifted slowly, as if weighted, and her gaze met his. He saw the passion that smoked her blue eyes, as well as the wonder.

Aroused by one and humbled by the other, he swept the pad of his thumb beneath her eye. "That's why I was afraid someone might come gunning for me. I wanted to kiss you and was afraid I had no right."

And he was afraid, too, if she kept looking at him like she was now, he'd wind up doing more than kiss her…

* * * * * *

Your opinion is important to us! Please take a few moments to share your thoughts with us about your experiences with Harlequin and Silhouette books. Your comments will be very useful in ensuring that we deliver books you love to read. ***Please take a few minutes to complete the questionnaire, then send it to us at the address below.***

Send your completed questionnaires to:
Harlequin/Silhouette Reader Survey, P.O. Box 9046, Buffalo, NY 14269-9046

1. As you may know, there are many different lines under the Harlequin and Silhouette brands. Each of the lines is listed below. Please check the box that most represents your reading habit for each line.

Line	Currently read this line	Do not read this line	Not sure if I read this line
Harlequin American Romance	❑	❑	❑
Harlequin Duets	❑	❑	❑
Harlequin Romance	❑	❑	❑
Harlequin Historicals	❑	❑	❑
Harlequin Superromance	❑	❑	❑
Harlequin Intrigue	❑	❑	❑
Harlequin Presents	❑	❑	❑
Harlequin Temptation	❑	❑	❑
Harlequin Blaze	❑	❑	❑
Silhouette Special Edition	❑	❑	❑
Silhouette Romance	❑	❑	❑
Silhouette Intimate Moments	❑	❑	❑
Silhouette Desire	❑	❑	❑

2. Which of the following best describes why you bought *this book?* One answer only, please.

the picture on the cover	❑	the title	❑
the author	❑	the line is one I read often	❑
part of a miniseries	❑	saw an ad in another book	❑
saw an ad in a magazine/newsletter	❑	a friend told me about it	❑
I borrowed/was given this book	❑	other: _____	❑

3. Where did you buy *this book?* One answer only, please.

at Barnes & Noble	❑	at a grocery store	❑
at Waldenbooks	❑	at a drugstore	❑
at Borders	❑	on eHarlequin.com Web site	❑
at another bookstore	❑	from another Web site	❑
at Wal-Mart	❑	Harlequin/Silhouette Reader Service/through the mail	❑
at Target	❑		
at Kmart	❑	used books from anywhere	❑
at another department store or mass merchandiser	❑	I borrowed/was given this book	❑

4. On average, how many Harlequin and Silhouette books do you buy at one time?

I buy _____ books at one time	❑
I rarely buy a book	❑

MRQ403SD-1A

5. How many times per month do you shop for any *Harlequin and/or Silhouette* books?
One answer only, please.

1 or more times a week	❑	a few times per year	❑
1 to 3 times per month	❑	less often than once a year	❑
1 to 2 times every 3 months	❑	never	❑

6. When you think of your ideal heroine, which *one* statement describes her the best?
One answer only, please.

She's a woman who is strong-willed	❑	She's a desirable woman	❑
She's a woman who is needed by others	❑	She's a powerful woman	❑
She's a woman who is taken care of	❑	She's a passionate woman	❑
She's an adventurous woman	❑	She's a sensitive woman	❑

7. The following statements describe types or genres of books that you may be
interested in reading. Pick *up to 2 types* of books that you are most interested in.

I like to read about truly romantic relationships	❑
I like to read stories that are sexy romances	❑
I like to read romantic comedies	❑
I like to read a romantic mystery/suspense	❑
I like to read about romantic adventures	❑
I like to read romance stories that involve family	❑
I like to read about a romance in times or places that I have never seen	❑
Other: _____	❑

*The following questions help us to group your answers with those readers who are
similar to you. Your answers will remain confidential.*

8. Please record your year of birth below.

19 ____

9. What is your marital status?

single ❑   married ❑   common-law ❑   widowed ❑
divorced/separated ❑

10. Do you have children 18 years of age or younger currently living at home?

yes ❑   no ❑

11. Which of the following best describes your employment status?

employed full-time or part-time ❑   homemaker ❑   student ❑
retired ❑   unemployed ❑

12. Do you have access to the Internet from either home or work?

yes ❑   no ❑

13. Have you ever visited eHarlequin.com?

yes ❑   no ❑

14. What state do you live in?

_____

15. Are you a member of Harlequin/Silhouette Reader Service?

yes ❑   Account # _____   no ❑   MRQ403SD-1B

Is your man too good to be true?

Hot, gorgeous AND romantic?
If so, he could be a Harlequin® Blaze™ series cover model!

Our grand-prize winners will receive a trip for two to New York City to shoot the cover of a Blaze novel, and will stay at the luxurious Plaza Hotel. Plus, they'll receive $500 U.S. spending money! The runner-up winners will receive $200 U.S. to spend on a romantic dinner for two.

It's easy to enter!

In 100 words or less, tell us what makes your boyfriend or spouse a true romantic and the perfect candidate for the cover of a Blaze novel, and include in your submission two photos of this potential cover model.

All entries must include the written submission of the contest entrant, two photographs of the model candidate and the Official Entry Form and Publicity Release forms completed in full and signed by both the model candidate and the contest entrant. Harlequin, along with the experts at Elite Model Management, will select a winner.

For photo and complete Contest details, please refer to the Official Rules on the next page. All entries will become the property of Harlequin Enterprises Ltd. and are not returnable.

Please visit www.blazecovermodel.com to download a copy of the Official Entry Form and Publicity Release Form or send a request to one of the addresses below.

Please mail your entry to: **Harlequin Blaze Cover Model Search**

In U.S.A.	In Canada
P.O. Box 9069	P.O. Box 637
Buffalo, NY	Fort Erie, ON
14269-9069	L2A 5X3

No purchase necessary. Contest open to Canadian and U.S. residents who are 18 and over. Void where prohibited. Contest closes September 30, 2003.

HARLEQUIN® **Blaze**™

HBCVRMODEL1

HARLEQUIN BLAZE COVER MODEL SEARCH CONTEST 3569 OFFICIAL RULES
NO PURCHASE NECESSARY TO ENTER

1. To enter, submit two (2) 4" x 6" photographs of a boyfriend or spouse (who must be 18 years of age or older) taken no later than three (3) months from the time of entry: a close-up, waist up, shirtless photograph; and a fully clothed, full-length photograph, then, tell us, in 100 words or fewer, why he should be a Harlequin Blaze cover model and how he is romantic. Your complete "entry" must include: (i) your essay, (ii) the Official Entry Form and Publicity Release Form printed below completed and signed by you (as "Entrant"), (iii) the photographs (with your hand-written name, address and phone number, and your model's name, address and phone number on the back of each photograph), and (iv) the Publicity Release Form and Photograph Representation Form printed below completed and signed by your model (as "Model"), and should be sent via first-class mail to either: Harlequin Blaze Cover Model Search Contest 3569, P.O. Box 9069, Buffalo, NY, 14269-9069, or Harlequin Blaze Cover Model Search Contest 3569, P.O. Box 637, Fort Erie, Ontario L2A 5X3. All submissions must be in English and be received no later than September 30, 2003. Limit: one entry per person, household or organization. **Purchase or acceptance of a product offer does not improve your chances of winning.** All entry requirements must be strictly adhered to for eligibility and to ensure fairness among entries.

2. Ten (10) Finalist submissions (photographs and essays) will be selected by a panel of judges consisting of members of the Harlequin editorial, marketing and public relations staff, as well as a representative from Elite Model Management (Toronto) Inc., based on the following criteria:

Aptness/Appropriateness of submitted photographs for a Harlequin Blaze cover—70%
Originality of Essay—20%
Sincerity of Essay—10%

In the event of a tie, duplicate finalists will be selected. The photographs submitted by finalists will be posted on the Harlequin website no later than November 15, 2003 (at www.blazecovermodel.com), and viewers may vote, in rank order, on their favorite(s) to assist in the panel of judges' final determination of the Grand Prize and Runner-up winning entries based on the above judging criteria. All decisions of the judges are final.

3. All entries become the property of Harlequin Enterprises Ltd. and none will be returned. Any entry may be used for future promotional purposes. Elite Model Management (Toronto) Inc. and/or its partners, subsidiaries and affiliates operating as "Elite Model Management" will have access to all entries including all personal information, and may contact any Entrant and/or Model in its sole discretion for their own business purposes. Harlequin and Elite Model Management (Toronto) Inc. are separate entities with no legal association or partnership whatsoever having no power to bind or obligate the other or create any expressed or implied obligation or responsibility on behalf of the other, such that Harlequin shall not be responsible in any way for any acts or omissions of Elite Model Management (Toronto) Inc. or its partners, subsidiaries and affiliates in connection with the Contest or otherwise and Elite Model Management shall not be responsible in any way for any acts or omissions of Harlequin or its partners, subsidiaries and affiliates in connection with the contest or otherwise.

4. All Entrants and Models must be residents of the U.S. or Canada, be 18 years of age or older, and have no prior criminal convictions. The contest is not open to any Model that is a professional model and/or actor in any capacity at the time of the entry. Contest void wherever prohibited by law; all applicable laws and regulations apply. Any litigation within the Province of Quebec regarding the conduct or organization of a publicity contest may be submitted to the Régie des alcools, des courses et des jeux for a ruling, and any litigation regarding the awarding of a prize may be submitted to the Régie only for the purpose of helping the parties reach a settlement. Employees and immediate family members of Harlequin Enterprises Ltd., D.L. Blair, Inc., Elite Model Management (Toronto) Inc. and their parents, affiliates, subsidiaries and all other agencies, entities and persons connected with the use, marketing or conduct of this Contest are not eligible to enter. Acceptance of any prize offered constitutes permission to use Entrants' and Models' names, essay submissions, photographs or other likenesses for the purposes of advertising, trade, publication and promotion on behalf of Harlequin Enterprises Ltd., its parent, affiliates, subsidiaries, assigns and other authorized entities involved in the judging and promotion of the contest without further compensation to any Entrant or Model, unless prohibited by law.

5. Finalists will be determined no later than October 30, 2003. Prize Winners will be determined no later than January 31, 2004. Grand Prize Winners (consisting of winning Entrant and Model) will be required to sign and return Affidavit of Eligibility/Release of Liability and Model Release forms within thirty (30) days of notification. Non-compliance with this requirement and within the specified time period will result in disqualification and an alternate will be selected. Any prize notification returned as undeliverable will result in the awarding of the prize to an alternate set of winners. All travelers (or parent/legal guardian of a minor) must execute the Affidavit of Eligibility/Release of Liability prior to ticketing and must possess required travel documents (e.g. valid photo ID) where applicable. Travel dates specified by Sponsor but no later than May 30, 2004.

6. Prizes: One (1) Grand Prize—the opportunity for the Model to appear on the cover of a paperback book from the Harlequin Blaze series, and a 3 day/2 night trip for two (Entrant and Model) to New York, NY for the photo shoot of Model which includes round-trip coach air transportation from the commercial airport nearest the winning Entrant's home to New York, NY, (or, in lieu of air transportation, $100 cash payable to Entrant and Model, if the winning Entrant's home is within 250 miles of New York, NY), hotel accommodations (double occupancy) at the Plaza Hotel and $500 cash spending money payable to Entrant and Model, (approximate prize value: $8,000), and one (1) Runner-up Prize of $200 cash payable to Entrant and Model for a romantic dinner for two (approximate prize value: $200). Prizes are valued in U.S. currency. Prizes consist of only those items listed as part of the prize. No substitution of prize(s) permitted by winners. All prizes are awarded jointly to the Entrant and Model of the winning entries, and are not severable - prizes and obligations may not be assigned or transferred. Any change to the Entrant and/or Model of the winning entries will result in disqualification and an alternate will be selected. Taxes on prize are the sole responsibility of winners. Any and all expenses and/or items not specifically described as part of the prize are the sole responsibility of winners. Harlequin Enterprises Ltd. and D.L. Blair, Inc., their parents, affiliates, and subsidiaries are not responsible for errors in printing of Contest entries and/or game pieces. No responsibility is assumed for lost, stolen, late, illegible, incomplete, inaccurate, non-delivered, postage due or misdirected mail or entries. In the event of printing or other errors which may result in unintended prize values or duplication of prizes, all affected game pieces or entries shall be null and void.

7. Winners will be notified by mail. For winners' list (available after March 31, 2004), send a self-addressed, stamped envelope to: Harlequin Blaze Cover Model Search Contest 3569 Winners, P.O. Box 4200, Blair, NE 68009-4200, or refer to the Harlequin website (at www.blazecovermodel.com).

Contest sponsored by Harlequin Enterprises Ltd., P.O. Box 9042, Buffalo, NY 14269-9042.

HBCVRMODEL2

If you enjoyed what you just read,
then we've got an offer you can't resist!

Take 2 bestselling
love stories FREE!
Plus get a FREE surprise gift!

Clip this page and mail it to Silhouette Reader Service™

IN U.S.A.
3010 Walden Ave.
P.O. Box 1867
Buffalo, N.Y. 14240-1867

IN CANADA
P.O. Box 609
Fort Erie, Ontario
L2A 5X3

YES! Please send me 2 free Silhouette Desire® novels and my free surprise gift. After receiving them, if I don't wish to receive anymore, I can return the shipping statement marked cancel. If I don't cancel, I will receive 6 brand-new novels every month, before they're available in stores! In the U.S.A., bill me at the bargain price of $3.57 plus 25¢ shipping and handling per book and applicable sales tax, if any*. In Canada, bill me at the bargain price of $4.24 plus 25¢ shipping and handling per book and applicable taxes**. That's the complete price and a savings of at least 10% off the cover prices—what a great deal! I understand that accepting the 2 free books and gift places me under no obligation ever to buy any books. I can always return a shipment and cancel at any time. Even if I never buy another book from Silhouette, the 2 free books and gift are mine to keep forever.

225 SDN DNUP
326 SDN DNUQ

Name	(PLEASE PRINT)	
Address	Apt.#	
City	State/Prov.	Zip/Postal Code

* Terms and prices subject to change without notice. Sales tax applicable in N.Y.
** Canadian residents will be charged applicable provincial taxes and GST.
   All orders subject to approval. Offer limited to one per household and not valid to current Silhouette Desire® subscribers.
   ® are registered trademarks of Harlequin Books S.A., used under license.

DES02   ©1998 Harlequin Enterprises Limited

COMING NEXT MONTH

#1537 MAN IN CONTROL—Diana Palmer
Long, Tall Texans
Undercover agent Alexander Cobb joined forces with his sworn
enemy Jodie Clayburn to crack a case. Surprisingly, working together
proved to be the easy part. The trouble they faced was fighting the
fiery attraction that threatened to consume them both!

#1538 BORN TO BE WILD—Anne Marie Winston
Dynasties: The Barones
Celia Papleo had been just a girl when Reese Barone sailed out of
her life, leaving her heart shattered. But now she was all woman—
and more than a match for the wealthy man who tempted her again.
Could a night of passion erase the misunderstandings of the past?

#1539 TEMPTING THE TYCOON—Cindy Gerard
Helping women find their happily-ever-afters was wedding planner
Rachel Matthew's trade. But she refused to risk her own heart. That
didn't stop roguishly charming millionaire lawyer Nate McGrory
from wanting to claim her for himself…and envisioning her icy
facade turing to molten lava at his touch!

#1540 LONETREE RANCHERS: MORGAN—Kathie DeNosky
Owning the most successful ranch in Wyoming was
Morgan Wakefield's dream. And it was now within his grasp—as
long as he wed Samantha Peterson. Their marriage was strictly a
business arrangement—but it didn't stem the desire they felt when
together….

#1541 HAVING THE BEST MAN'S BABY—Shawna Delacorte
For Jean Summerfield, the one thing worse than having to wear a
bridesmaid dress was facing her unreliable ex, best man Ry Collier.
But Jean's dormant desire sparked to life at Ry's touch. Would Ry
stay to face the consequences of their passion, or leave her burned
once more?

**#1542 COWBOY'S MILLION-DOLLAR SECRET—
Emilie Rose**
Charismatic cowboy Patrick Lander knew exactly who he was—
until virginal beauty Leanna Jensen brought news that Patrick
would inherit his biological father's multimillion-dollar estate! The
revelation threw Patrick's settled life into chaos—but paled compared
to the emotions Leanna aroused in him.

SDCNM0903